SELECT PRAISE FOR
Norman Lock's American Novels Series

"Shimmers with glorious language, fluid rhythms, and complex insights."
—**NPR**

"Our national history and literature are Norman Lock's playground in his dazzling series, The American Novels. . . . [His] supple, elegantly plain-spoken prose captures the generosity of the American spirit in addition to its moral failures, and his passionate engagement with our literary heritage evinces pride in its unique character."
—*Washington Post*

"This is fiction of a high caliber . . . on the cutting edge of history, providing us with a way to grapple with our evolving sense of the past, as we wonder what is next."
—*New York Sun*

"Lock writes some of the most deceptively beautiful sentences in contemporary fiction. Beneath their clarity are layers of cultural and literary references, profound questions about loyalty, race, the possibility of social progress, and the nature of truth . . . to create something entirely new—an American fable of ideas."
—*Shelf Awareness*

"[A] consistently excellent series. . . . Lock has an impressive ear for the musicality of language, and his characteristic lush prose brings vitality and poetic authenticity to the dialogue."
—*Booklist*

On *The Boy in His Winter*

"[Lock] is one of the most interesting writers out there. This time, he re-imagines Huck Finn's journeys, transporting the iconic character deep into America's past—and future."
—*Reader's Digest*

On *American Meteor*

"[Walt Whitman] hovers over [*American Meteor*], just as Mark Twain's spirit pervaded *The Boy in His Winter*. . . . Like all Mr. Lock's books, this is an ambitious work, where ideas crowd together on the page like desperate men on a battlefield."
—*Wall Street Journal*

On *The Port-Wine Stain*

"Lock's novel engages not merely with [Edgar Allan Poe and Thomas Dent Mütter] but with decadent fin de siècle art and modernist literature that raised philosophical and moral questions about the metaphysical relations among art, science and human consciousness. The reader is just as spellbound by Lock's story as [his novel's narrator] is by Poe's. . . . Echoes of Wilde's *The Picture of Dorian Gray* and Freud's theory of the uncanny abound in this mesmerizingly twisted, richly layered homage to a pioneer of American Gothic fiction."
—*New York Times Book Review*

On *A Fugitive in Walden Woods*

"*A Fugitive in Walden Woods* manages that special magic of making Thoreau's time in Walden Woods seem fresh and surprising and necessary right now. . . . This is a patient and perceptive novel, a pleasure to read even as it grapples with issues that affect the United States to this day."
—**Victor LaValle**

On *The Wreckage of Eden*

"The lively passages of Emily [Dickinson]'s letters are so evocative of her poetry that it becomes easy to see why Robert finds her so captivating. The book also expands and deepens themes of moral hypocrisy around racism and slavery. . . . Lyrically written but unafraid of the ugliness of the time, Lock's thought-provoking series continues to impress."
—*Publishers Weekly*

On *Feast Day of the Cannibals*

"Lock does not merely imitate 19th-century prose; he makes it his own, with verbal flourishes worthy of Melville."
—*Gay & Lesbian Review*

On *American Follies*

"*Ragtime* in a fever dream. . . . When you mix 19th-century racists, feminists, misogynists, freaks, and a flim-flam man, the spectacle that results might bear resemblance to the contemporary United States."
—*Library Journal* **(starred review)**

On *Tooth of the Covenant*

"Splendid. . . . Lock masters the interplay between nineteenth-century Hawthorne and his fictional surrogate, Isaac, as he travels through Puritan New England. The historical details are immersive and meticulous."
—*Foreword Reviews* **(starred review)**

On *Voices in the Dead House*

"Gripping. . . . The legacy of John Brown looms over both Alcott and Whitman [in] a haunting novel that offers candid portraits of literary legends."
—*Kirkus Reviews* **(starred review)**

On *The Ice Harp*

"Lock deftly takes us into the polyphonic swirl of Emerson's mind at the end of his life, inviting us to meet the man anew even as the philosopher fights to stop forgetting himself. . . . [A] remarkably empathetic and deeply moral novel."
—**Matt Bell**

On *The Caricaturist*

"Lock successfully mimics Crane's impressionistic style in his marvelous depictions of late 19th-century America."
—*Publishers Weekly*

Eden's Clock

The Complete American Novels Series

Eden's Clock
The Caricaturist
The Ice Harp
Voices in the Dead House
The Tooth of the Covenant
American Follies
Feast Day of the Cannibals
The Wreckage of Eden
A Fugitive in Walden Woods
The Port-Wine Stain
American Meteor
The Boy in His Winter

Also by Norman Lock

Love Among the Particles (stories)

Eden's Clock

Norman Lock

Bellevue Literary Press
New York

First published in the United States in 2025
by Bellevue Literary Press, New York

For information, contact:
Bellevue Literary Press
90 Broad Street
Suite 2100
New York, NY 10004
www.blpress.org

© 2025 by Norman Lock

This is a work of fiction. Characters, organizations, events, and places (even those that are actual) are either products of the author's imagination or are used fictitiously.

Library of Congress Cataloging-in-Publication Data
Names: Lock, Norman, author.
Title: Eden's clock / Norman Lock.
Description: First edition. | New York : Bellevue Literary Press, 2025. | Series: The American novels
Identifiers: LCCN 2025000211 | ISBN 9781954276383 (paperback ; acid-free paper) | ISBN 9781954276390 (epub)
Subjects: LCSH: Veterans--Fiction. | Clock and watch makers--Fiction. | United States--History--20th century--Fiction. | San Francisco Earthquake and Fire, Calif., 1906--Fiction. | LCGFT: Historical fiction. | Novels.
Classification: LCC PS3562.O218 E34 2025 | DDC 813/.54--dc23/eng/20250103

LC record available at https://lccn.loc.gov/2025000211

All rights reserved. No part of this publication may be reproduced or transmitted in any form or by any means, electronic or mechanical, including photocopy, recording, or any information storage and retrieval system now known or to be invented, without permission in writing from the publisher, except by a reviewer who wishes to quote brief passages in connection with a print, online, or broadcast review. No part of this book may be used or reproduced in any manner for the purpose of training artificial intelligence technologies or systems.

Bellevue Literary Press would like to thank all its generous donors—individuals and foundations—for their support.

 This publication is made possible by the New York State Council on the Arts with the support of the Office of the Governor and the New York State Legislature.

Book design and composition by Mulberry Tree Press, Inc.

Bellevue Literary Press is committed to ecological stewardship in our book production practices, working to reduce our impact on the natural environment.

∞ This book is printed on acid-free paper.

Manufactured in the United States of America.

First Edition

10 9 8 7 6 5 4 3 2 1

paperback ISBN: 978-1-954276-38-3
ebook ISBN: 978-1-954276-39-0

To My Teachers
Mildred Osler, Daniel Hoffman, Philip Roth,
George P. Elliott, Philip Booth, Gordon Lish,
and Charles Giraudet

*I had been reborn, but not renamed,
and I was running around to find out
what manner of thing I was.*

—"How I Became a Socialist,"
Jack London, 1903

*Facing west from California's shores,
Inquiring, tireless, seeking what is yet unfound, . . .*

—Walt Whitman

Westward the Course of Empire takes its way;
The first four Acts already past,
A fifth shall close the Drama with the Day . . .

—Bishop Berkeley,
"Verses on the Prospect of Planting Arts
and Learning in America," 1726

Desolation, Thomas Cole, 1836
(from *The Course of Empire* series)

Eden's Clock

The Palace Hotel Bar

THE NIGHT OF APRIL 17, 1906,
ABOUT ELEVEN O'CLOCK
SAN FRANCISCO

EDITH WELLER HAD EMBARKED for San Francisco at Des Moines to hear her beloved Caruso sing at the Grand Opera House of the city of the seven hills. She missed his performance of Don José, in Bizet's opera *Carmen*, by a few hours. As we stood outside the silent, shut-up building hulking in the shadows of Mission Street, she refused to give the Furies the satisfaction of so much as a trembling lip. They had pursued her all the way from Iowa, loosed by a husband who considered the great tenor a "queer customer even for a foreigner," and her behavior disgraceful for the wife of an officer of the Bank of Prairie City. She clenched her teeth in anger at unreliable railway schedules and had a few choice words for the Almighty, who might have spared her a thought, while He was feeding the sparrows, although she allowed that He may not care much for French opera. Her language would not have caused one of your Klondike bad men to spit tobacco like a grasshopper taken by

17

18   NORMAN LOCK

surprise, but it would have ruffled aigrette feathers in Prairie City. You'd like Edith Weller, Mr. London. She's the sort of woman who doesn't give two pins for doilies and would never think of carrying smelling salts. She'd sooner throw on a rubber coat and keep you company in the snow than swoon.

I smiled a good night to Edith and drifted down the street to the Palace Hotel taproom, where, it turned out, you were doing some fine cussing of your own. Now I'm sitting at a table next to yours, listening to you air your views on social inequity to your three comrades. I wish I could tell you about the "socialists" I met by the East River. They're worth a story, Mr. London, and so are the grifters, hawkers, hucksters, breakers, do-gooders, and broken men I bumped into on the way out here from Dobbs Ferry, New York. But I'm a mute and have been one since the Civil War wrung my neck of the last syllable of the last word that Fred Heigold would utter on this Earth.

I'm a clocksmith and would be in Dobbs Ferry plying my trade had my wife not fallen down the stairs. For forty years, my pleasure was to lay bare a universe in miniature, whose only complications were the minute machinery that contrived to chime the hour or show the phases of the moon on a painted dial surrounded by a metal bezel. I seldom stopped to marvel at the grand rotations of the stars and planets, but the clockwork movement, where time is

Eden's Clock 19

bound like Ixion to a fiery wheel, held no mystery for me. To my mind and in my expert hands, time was clear and straightforward, like water running from a tap. I understood that a gear's worn tooth or a particle of grit wreaked havoc with the works, but the forces that have been marshaled against the order of my days cannot be explained by horology. The savage element we thought, in our vanity, to have been civilized by a timetable has stripped off its gloves and soon will take us by the throat. I've read enough of your tales, Mr. London, to know what you think of existence: All that stands between a man and his death is a fire to keep the frost and wolves at bay and a dry match to light it.

I think that the snow that falls on my neighbor's cat remembers, in its atoms, falling on the mastodon during the Ice Age, which waits, in the depth of winter, to engulf us once more. I did not always have such gloomy thoughts, Mr. London—I'll call you Jack, shall I? We've met, though you won't remember me. I was one of four thousand admirers at New York City's Grand Central Palace who heard you speak on "The Coming Crisis." Afterward, my late wife, Lilian, conspicuous that night for the red badge of the Socialist Party of America pinned to her coat, was among a pack of women het up on prison reform who cornered you to praise your outspokenness in defense of the poor and downtrodden. You shook our hands. I felt the strength that had broken jaws on the Barbary Coast, driven sled dogs in the Hills of Silence, and reefed sails in the Bering Strait on the way to Japan.

And now here you are, at the table next to mine, one meaty hand around the throat of a beer bottle, the other raking a wayward hank of brown hair from your forehead. You have just finished interviewing Maestro Caruso for *Collier's Weekly* magazine, in the Palace's best room. At this moment, Edith Weller is standing at the window of a far less opulent hotel, looking down Market Street toward the Embarcadero, where the Union Depot tower clock looms, moonlike, in the yellow fog. Or so I imagine her leaning against the window sash, worn out and let down after traveling fifteen hundred miles to hear her musical idol sing.

The Union Depot clock is the reason I've come to San Francisco, at the invitation of Herbert Wallace, the man in charge of the city's public works. The great clock does not keep proper time, and nothing would do but that Frederick Heigold of Dobbs Ferry must set it right. I have, you see, a certain fame of my own.

Jack, you've been to sea and know that if a ship strays off course by so much as a degree of latitude, it can end up at the world's bitter end. Every second counts, as is said and I believed until my anabasis stood a clocksmith's logic on its head. I still give time its due; that much hasn't changed since I left New York last fall. But increasingly, I feel like your nearly

Eden's Clock   21

frozen man in the Yukon, who managed to build a fire with his last match, only to melt the snow on a branch above his head, extinguishing the fire and himself. Our kind is readily undone; we're down to our last match and a thousand miles north of home.

I could as easily be drinking rum in a Cuban *taberna* with my friend Mr. Bonaparte as enjoying a quiet drink near a man whose books I admire— quiet for me, who can't speak a word, though not for you, who have turned from castigating Rockefeller and Frick to the story of your conversion to socialism. You are talking to three others; they are, like you, hard-drinking young men sharing a devil-may-care attitude toward what most of us consider holy. Rainier beer bottles stand in broken formation, one fallen on its side, their tin hats scattered on the sticky table, where a solitary fly rubs its forelegs in satisfaction.

Most people think of timepieces as a constant reminder of our mortal span. For me, they were a comfort. Each clock and pocket watch I took apart and put together again was a triumph over time, however small. I saw myself as someone with the skill to take its measure, if not to bend it to my will. That ascendancy was my consolation for the inevitable defeat time will deal me and us all. Intent on a piece of clockwork, I took no notice of anything else. It was a dainty cosmos, humble in ambition, but as fascinating as anything in the firmament that the Herschels beheld through their telescopes. How could I not have loved it—and feared it, as well?

Now I know time for what it is: slow death. I'm freer knowing it, and yet I miss the way I used to be—a cog. No, *cog* is not exactly right. I had a body that felt and a mind that saw beyond the machinery, a little way beyond it. Let's say I was a partner in a dance. There is pain when the music stops and the woman on your arm takes that of another man, pain when the mechanism falls to pieces. You're torn loose and on your own. I may never have known this pain had Lilian not died before me, never left Dobbs Ferry. I'd have been content to be time's mechanic and let her do the talking for the two of us.

Eavesdropping, I hear you tell your fellow scribblers about the first time you went east, in '94, with the Industrial Army of the United States, raised in Oakland by the San Francisco printer and student of sociology Charles Kelly, purposing to join Jacob Coxey's so-called Army of the Unemployed, in Washington, for a May Day demonstration, demanding jobs during that year of starving after the great panic. No sooner did Coxey and his men approach the Capitol than they were jailed for walking on the lawn. His soldiers, hungry and broken, straggled home. Dispirited, "General" Kelly's retreated to the western states, while you, Jack, went on to Chicago and thence to

Eden's Clock   23

New York City. Your course, like mine during these last six months, has been erratic.

"I found there all sorts of men, many of whom had once been as good as myself and just as blond-beast; sailor-men, soldier-men, labor-men, all wrenched and distorted and twisted out of shape by toil and hardship and accident, and cast adrift by their masters like so many old horses. I battered on the drag and slammed back gates with them, or shivered with them in box cars and city parks, listening the while to life-histories which began under auspices as fair as mine, with digestions and bodies equal to and better than mine, and which ended there before my eyes in the shambles at the bottom of the Social Pit."

If not for the chance encounter of a half-ounce lead ball and my larynx, I would tell you and your comrades that it takes only a misstep to end up at the bottom of the stairs. Moreover, I would have arrived in the City of the Golden Gate six months ago, if the machinery by which we appear to govern the universe and ourselves had not gone haywire. In the frustration felt by those who cannot speak their minds, I upset my glass of beer.

You glance my way before continuing: "The woman of the streets and the man of the gutter drew very close to me. I saw the picture of the Social Pit as vividly as though it were a concrete thing, and at the bottom of the Pit I saw them, myself above them, not far, and hanging on to the slippery wall by main strength and sweat. I confess a terror seized me. What when my strength failed?"

Then you'll go under with the rest, I reply in my mind, which has grown cynical. I can't very well scribble the answer on the bill of fare and drop it on your plate. Nor can I tell you the complicated story of my own adventure, which began in a New York State village on the east bank of the Hudson River, twenty miles north of Manhattan's Battery, and ended tonight on San Francisco's Market Street, while Caruso snores operatically on the fifth floor above my head.

Had I a voice, and you, Jack, the inclination to hear me, I would tell the following story.

OCTOBER 1905–JANUARY 1906

1

LILIAN, ALWAYS ON THE BOIL over wrongs done to the least of us—she, too, was rendered speechless when, coming down to start breakfast, she stumbled on the stairs. I heard a gasp of astonishment and then a thud as her body came to rest on the floor and she started on her afterlife. I let out a wordless scream, as a dumb animal might make in the slaughter pen. So terrible the strain of it, I thought my ribs would crack. Had I the power of speech, that scream would have swamped the morning boat from Tarrytown, then traveled up the Hudson River, by the laws governing such things, and shaken the stone walls of Sing Sing, bringing convicts to their knees to confess their sins, on the advent of Judgment Day.

I ran next door to the Germans' house, forgetting my slate and chalk. Lacking the means to make myself understood, I pulled Kopf rudely by the sleeve, through the hedge separating our two properties, up onto the porch, and into the parlor, where Lilian had not moved an inch. From then on, a hairsbreadth would be as impossible for her to cross as a continent—that good woman who was never, in her life, still. She was, she said, born wearing a pair of walking shoes, and was never so fired up as when she paraded in her bloomers, in a troop of reformers devoted to justice and lost causes. As Kopf covered her face with the Dobbs Ferry *Register*, I stood amazed by the absence of her voice, which, for forty-two years, had been obliged to speak for me, as well as for herself.

Often, when I have stopped in the middle of something and am straining to recall voices from that grief-struck house, I hear only those of Lucius Clay, the unctuous embalmer, and his lummox of a son. They appeared at the deathbed, as if out of thin air, bearing a tailor's tape to take Lilian's measurements and a crepe band for the brand-new widower's sleeve. Two days later, I was buried in sympathy and, from the town's righteous nitwits, in admonitions against letting myself go. "Buck up, Heigold! To everything there is a season." To suck the bitter tooth of remorse, to wallow in guilt for neglecting the ruckled carpet on the stair are an insult to God, by whose divine will Lilian fell and broke her neck.

Is it never His will that we should escape, if only by the skin of our teeth, the fall that seems our lot always to suffer? Couldn't she have flown safely down the stairs by a miraculous instance of divine intervention or, at least, have found her footing? What husband whose wife has gone before him to the grave has not wondered why it must be so?

Lilian was older than I, and stronger. Less of a woman would not have had the strength or the grit to unearth me from my homemade grave. Even now, across a gulf of time, I can see her standing over me with her arms crossed, stern and formidable in her nurse's uniform and cap. She'd heard about "the bad case of the sulks" who had lost his voice in Virginia, at Manassas Gap. She was neither kith nor kin to me, but she refused to let me stew in my own juices, on a cot in Union Hospital. The wards were filled with men who'd given their legs and arms to the surgeon's saw; I'd lost only my voice.

"Mr. Heigold, would you rather be dead, maimed, or dumb?"

After only the briefest of hesitations, which may have been for show, I indicated the last course on that grim menu of human woe.

Lilian had made her point.

2

I was a corporal in the Sixtieth New York Volunteer Infantry. Robert E. Lee's Army of Northern Virginia had taken a terrible beating on the first, second, and third of July 1863. I was at the "fish hook" on the

28   NORMAN LOCK

third, the turning point in the Battle of Gettysburg, when the Union army repulsed a massive assault on Culp's Hill. Twenty-two thousand men, blue and gray, fought over two peaks and the saddle between them. We would've finished off Lee's army and ended the war then and there if the Draft Riots hadn't compelled General Meade to detach four thousand men from his main force at Gettysburg to subdue the Irish in New York City.

Lee's weary and bedraggled army was able to retreat across the Potomac into northern Virginia. Meade attempted to flank it by sending III Corps, under Major General French, across the river at Harper's Ferry and on into the Loudoun Valley of the Blue Ridge Mountains. Our advance stalled at Manassas Gap on July 23. We held Front Royal, but not before the butternuts had slipped farther up the Shenandoah Valley. They regrouped and lived to fight another day—626 days, to be exact, as a clocksmith must. July 23 also marked my last as a man who could speak his own mind.

The year before Gettysburg, the battle that proved to be the salvation of the Union, I'd been with the Sixtieth at Antietam, Maryland, called Sharpsburg south of the Mason-Dixon line. Seventeen thousand Union and Confederate men and boys were wounded in that single blood-soaked day. I went all to pieces in Miller's cornfield when the "Louisiana Tigers" broke our back along Hagerstown Turnpike, on the seventeenth of September 1862.

Mr. Lincoln came up from Washington City to review the grisly aftermath and chew the ears off McClellan, who wasn't worth a fart in a fight. He was a show general, much admired on the parade ground by gents who would never trade their yellow shoes for cardboard boots, their frock coats for shoddy. I recall the president and McClellan in a white tent, sitting opposite each other on camp chairs; neither looked pleased. The tall, lean man was downcast before the small, smug one. Abe had not yet begun to age, which he would do, frightfully and soon.

After the war, I bought a secondhand copy of Gardner's picture album of the dead of Antietam. Struck by the notion that I might come across a picture of myself in a pile of dead men, I've never opened it. How strange are the thoughts that get into a man's brain and play havoc with his good sense!

Rubbing polish onto Lilian's coffin lid with a rag that had never soaked up a living man's blood, Brutus, the embalmer's witless son, confided that he'd had to break her leg to lay her out properly. So casual was his remark, he might have been talking about a limb sawn off a tree to improve the view. He may have been speaking his thoughts aloud, believing that I was deaf as well as dumb, a common mistake. Feeling a flush of blood, I clenched my fists and would have

30 NORMAN LOCK

liked to beat the dullard's brains out. But mourners would soon be at the door, where Lucius had hung a black beribboned wreath—much too large a one, in my estimation.

On the day I visited the Clays' establishment to make the funerary arrangements, Lucius boasted of his enlightened attitude toward mortuary practice. He showed off the latest in pumps and aspirators of German manufacture, the Köhler cooling board, a casket-lowering device, and he demonstrated the patented Chicago bicycle clipper, which, by furious pedaling, Brutus used to groom the horses. Later, I unwittingly offended Lucius when I mistook a crock of "Durfee's Best" for moonshine. With the indignation of a priest before a nonbeliever who scoffed at the mystery of transubstantiation, he produced a testimonial from his desk drawer in praise of the fluid's ability to slow the course of corruption:

> The body of Geo. S. Andrick was embalmed by us with Durfee Fluid, and was buried on the 15th day of September 1892, which is more than seven years before its exhumation and removal to another burial place; other bodies that have been removed from the same cemetery were in the usual state of decomposition. Not so that of Mr.

Andrick. We swear by Durfee Fluid for keeping our corpses looking fresh.

C. W. Morrison & Son,
Mortuarians, Greenfield, Ind.

I pantomimed an apology. His wounded pride salved, he favored me with a reading from *Ranch Tales of the Rockies*, by cowboy poet Harry Ellard, of the Cincinnati Coffin Company. I'll spare you the *clop, clop* of doggerel, Jack.

"That man can swing a rhyme as easily as he can a lariat!" said Lucius after his recitation.

On the day of Lilian's ceremonial departure, I opened the coffin's hatch and looked, for the last time, at the dear face. The brass hinge squawked, but dumb show was beyond me. Lucius stood by the open parlor door, ready to deal out raffia fans rubber-stamped with the name of the family firm and its "sacred promise of efficiency." The promise of eternity would have been more comforting, but as the undertaker had confided during my tour of the premises, "Ours is a highly competitive profession."

The minister of the Dobbs Ferry Second Methodist Church appeared, looking as if he'd spent an agreeable afternoon in 1692, examining Salem witches. Had I patience and sufficient chalk, I would have challenged his presence in my parlor, in that neither Lilian nor I had ever set foot in his church or, indeed, in any other church since our wedding day, having decided, mutually, that such wisdom as priests and pastors were likely to dispense was not worth wearing out our knees on kneeling benches. I could see from the way the man rearranged his features that he meant to descant on the bliss to come. I shook out my handkerchief and blew with so stentorian an effect that his overture was spoiled. Ignoring me, he turned to Kopf and related one of Ezekiel's grim prophecies. Silently, I wished him gone to hell.

Lilian liked to remind the righteous, who congregate like flies on a dung heap, that the devil is a man who lords it over women wearing stays. Together with her partners in impiety, Susan B. Anthony and Elizabeth Cady Stanton, author of that wicked work *The Woman's Bible*, she let her fierceness show as shamelessly as a certain kind of woman does her breasts. (Lilian would not have said *bosom*, nor would she have called a piano leg a limb.) Suffragists are no better than prostitutes in the eyes of men who revile the one and resort to the other.

Miss Anthony had sent me her famous red shawl to put around Lilian's shoulders for her long wintering in the ground, "among the turnips." The shawl went missing; I guessed that the staunch Republicans of the village insisted that the Clays "burn the damn rag," looking, as it did, like the socialist flag.

Eden's Clock   33

I wasn't a socialist, except as a clocksmith might be so inclined. The trade gives one to understand that every human, like every gear and gear's tooth, is essential to the running of the works, and therefore equal. I admit that I didn't take the lesson of the clockwork and apply it to men and women in society. Not in Dobbs Ferry. No one is born a socialist. Even you, Jack, had to knock around some before you could see that the paradise of your father's ranch wasn't the way of the world.

Kopf and I, together with Clay the father and Clay the son, carried Lilian, boxed up for good, through death's door in the vestibule, which, in lively times, contained a coat tree and an umbrella stand. The wall's porcelain tiles were sallow, like old piano keys, which would have made a doleful music being struck. The mourners, their faces betraying more grumpiness than sorrow, left the house by the front door, leaving behind Mrs. Kopf's damask napkins stained not with tears of grief but with blueberry buckle. The sweet had been set out on my kitchen table, along with cups of cider, to fortify the funeral party. We slid the casket into the hearse, over a patented roller affair, which wanted oiling, like the coffin hatch. The sun, fickle on that October morning, became entangled in a fine net of cracks in the hearse's larboard window, as Herman Melville would say, were he still among the living.

3

Melville had been on my mind that morning as I walked along the ferry slips. The sun was in a somber mood, to match my own, and the gray chop of the Hudson made me think of him and what he may have felt, embarking on his first voyage from a wharf in New York City, and—if the recently departed feel anything at all—on his final one from Woodlawn Cemetery, near Old Fordham Village in the Bronx. The all but forgotten novelist had been recalled from obscurity, for me, when a young woman acquaintance of his had stopped with us in 1883. She had been taken ill on the train coming down from Sing Sing, traveling in the same car as Lilian. Ellen Finch was her name, an amiable woman, though somewhat broken in mind. She was in a terrible state when the railway porter wheeled her in a baggage truck to our front door. After her fever broke, I got to know her as much as someone with my limited means can know a stranger. I liked that she wasn't put out by my silence. She gave me her attention, while I held up my end of the conversation, which left traces of itself in the form of chalk dust on my sleeve, which I sometimes use as an eraser.

Lilian had become a champion of prison reform, after attending the National Conference of Charities

Eden's Clock 35

and Corrections in Louisville. It was another of her enthusiasms, which were many and mostly worthwhile. Twice a month, she traveled the twenty miles to Sing Sing and back to give spiritual comfort to the inmates, or so she claimed. In fact, her purpose in going there was to keep Mr. Brockway, the warden of Elmira Reformatory, informed of the harsh conditions behind the redbrick walls at Ossining, on the Upper Hudson. Along with a handful of other enlightened prison authorities, he advocated humane treatment of the incarcerated.

Walking beside the river that morning not long after Lilian's death, I recalled the day that she and I, along with our daughter, Louisa, named for Louisa May Alcott, who had befriended Lilian in Georgetown early in the war, took a southbound ferry to Spuyten Duyvil. From there, we traveled by streetcar to Woodlawn Cemetery. Although neither of us had met Melville, we went to pay our last respects at the request of Ellen Finch, who had known him in New York in the eighties. At the time of his death, in September 1891, Ellen had been living in San Francisco. Last year, she, too, left the land of the living after suffering the agony of meningitis.

At the graveside, a jackass of the human variety joked that Melville's burial was overdue, since the writer had been dead for thirty years. He had brought an obituary clipped from *The New York Times* and took a spiteful pleasure in quoting from it: "In its kind this speedy oblivion by which a once famous man so long survived his fame is almost unique." The burial service was conducted by Dr. Williams of All Souls' Church. A funeral supper was to follow at the Schnitzel Haus. Had Lilian not renounced stays, they would have crackled sympathetically in electric resentment. She said she would "rather suck a sour pickle than share a meal with men who've come to gloat!" We left the cemetery to the dead. In honor of the author of *Moby-Dick*, she and I gorged ourselves on oysters tonged up that morning from Pelham Bay. Louisa ate bread and butter washed down with sarsaparilla.

You are sure to have read his books, Jack, and I'd be interested in hearing your opinion of them. His prose is not so plain as yours, but you have a common interest in putting man at his wit's end.

On the way back to the ferry depot, I stopped at a bookseller's near the botanical garden. Of Melville's writings, I found only a mildewed copy of *Clarel: A Poem and Pilgrimage in the Holy Land*. The title discouraged me, who am not religious, except as anyone would be who stands in awe of what is greater than himself—in my case, time, an omnipotence to wonder at and fear. I bought a copy of *The Poetical Works of Samuel Taylor Coleridge*, bound in half leather. The white-domed conservancy rising above the botanical garden might have been decreed by Kublai Khan, although it had been paid for by Morgan, Rockefeller, and Carnegie to put a pretty face on their rapacity.

On the ferryboat home, I recalled the scroll carved onto Melville's stone; it was blank, as though waiting for him to reach out his hand from eternity and chisel a line of prose or verse that would explain God to man or man to God, or answer the age-old question why some people end their mortal term shaded by polished granite while others—so many others—thirst forever in a pauper's grave.

4

Time, opiate for the gnawing tooth of grief, has dampened the sound of earth raining on the lid of Lilian's coffin. Of that solemn afternoon, the rusty screech of a red-tailed hawk circling Croton Aqueduct, the shrill cry of the Tarrytown packet, and the chuffing of its steam engine—only those persist inside the vaulting bone. Besides the Kopfs, who stood on either side of me, in case I should give way, few turned out to condole or, more likely, ogle. Dobbs Ferry considered Lilian a crackpot suffragist who believed in *The Woman's Bible* instead of Holy Writ. Gossips buzzed behind her back, insinuating indecencies committed with the convicts during her visits to Sing Sing. The Bible bleaters of the town would have preferred that I bury her in Irvington, but none could argue against a deeded plot; property is sacred—none more so than that which exists in perpetuity, for the enjoyment of perennial bindweed and spurge.

Lilian's coffin stowed in the funeral coach, the small party of mourners made its slow progress up Broadway. Where the road veers north onto Ashford Avenue, we passed through the gates of the cemetery. The black coach rocked on its leaf springs. The black iron urns jerked on the roof. The black horses walked on, while black egret feathers trembled on their solemn heads as windblown shadows from the cypress trees swirled about us. The jumping-off point from this world to the next called to mind a train shed, its windows covered with soot. A shrill blast from the river's edge heralding the arrival of a Hudson River Railroad train enhanced the likeness.

We've been brought to the mouth of hell in a George L. Brownell funeral coach, I said to myself. I knew full well that neither of Dobbs Ferry's officious conductors would appreciate the comparison. How seriously men take themselves and their affairs! Lilian always found us, our sex, self-important and absurd. Having men in the saddle made her pessimistic. "Why, just think how long it took them to emancipate the slaves, who, being their equal in the eyes of their God, ought not to have required it! How long will it be until women, who must await the pleasure of white men in authority, can vote?" Her passion was not of the flammable sort; she came to a boil slowly. But once the lid began to knock, it took asbestos gloves to handle her. I've seen her pace the yard, beheading the irises with her hickory stick.

I refused to let the Reverend Hardy, of Second Methodist, speak. I could not forbid him entry into the sacred precincts of Dobbs Ferry's dead. He scowled at me during the obsequies presided over by my son-in-law, a Unitarian minister at Oberlin, who had come from Ohio for the purpose. Louisa had remained behind, her eighth-month belly risen like bread. Peter invited me to live with them in Oberlin or, if I were not prepared to surrender my independence, in a house of my own there. I flirted with the notion. But in the end, I wasn't ready to be known as Peter's father-in-law or Louisa's father. I had been Lilian's husband all our married life—the price a man pays who marries a strong woman and cannot say yea or nay for himself. When I lose my mind and become someone or something else, Dobbs Ferry has an asylum with a view of the lordly Hudson. Henry Kopf promised to visit and bring with him a generous piece of his wife's blueberry buckle.

I stayed behind with the untalkative dead, to think a few words that I had never spoken within her hearing. Like many another widowed man, I felt certain that, for a brief moment of the final parting, Lilian could hear my thoughts. I left her to her own and walked away from the raw wound of earth, through a crowd of pines, holly, and cypress trees, brightened, here and there, by rose of Sharon bushes and wild carrot. The dogwood trees were shedding their crimson leaves; I would not be there in the spring to see them flame above the new grass.

5

After the business of dying was concluded, I went from room to room to read the terse messages that I had written on the slates hung throughout the house. Not one rose above the commonplace; none expressed a sentiment worthy of remembrance. What turned out to be my last words to my wife the night before she died had to do with a loose button on my sleeve and pepper hash, with which I was fed up. I racked my brain to wring out from memory what she may have said to me as she went up to bed, the last time she would take the stairs under her own steam. I'd been too absorbed in your story "The Devil's Dice Box" to listen, Jack.

I have always read. What else is a solitary person to do? I make others uncomfortable. They cross the street rather than risk being greeted or, even more disconcerting, questioned by a chalkboard attached to a man. As I said, Lilian was the family *spokesman*— the word gave her fits. In time, Louisa went to the

Eden's Clock   41

grocer's, the emporium, or the stationer's, clutching a shopping list in her small hand. With no one left in the house, I went to the stores myself, list in hand, but the shopkeepers shied from me. It raised my hackles to be shunned. I knew then what poor put-upon Hester Prynne, who wore a scarlet letter, had suffered in old Salem for the love of craven Arthur Dimmesdale. I've read Milton's *Paradise Lost* and Hawthorne's tales, but I think they harp overmuch on sin. I prefer Shakespeare, who was not above the bawdy.

How I missed Lilian! I miss her now, if not so sorely. A wound will eventually scab over, until it is felt no more. (I suspect Hawthorne gnawed on his heart rather than let it grow callous.)

I remember an afternoon as we watched Louisa play with her cat. She asked her mother, "Why doesn't Mr. Bounderby ever talk?" That was her name for me, picked up from Dickens's book *Hard Times*, which Louisa was reading to her. "He's just like Merlin, who sits, licks his paw, and looks like he might make a remark, but never does."

"There's enough nonsense spouted in this world without either Merlin or Mr. Bounderby adding his two cents," replied Lilian, giving me a wink.

The night before her wedding to Peter, Louisa asked, as any daughter might, how Lilian and I came to meet and marry. She would have already known, but she wished to hear my side of it. ASK YOUR

42 NORMAN LOCK

MOTHER. Goodness, girl, you can't tell the story of your heart with a stick of chalk!

Later, I sat at the kitchen table, and in a circle of tawny light shed by the kerosene lamp, I wrote in answer to her question. Brevity becomes habitual in the mute, and my messages to the world tend to be telegraphic. But on that night, I filled several pages torn from my notebook. The words, as if freed after a long imprisonment, rushed out the narrow gate. I put the pages in the trunk in which Louisa would carry her worldly goods to Oberlin, to begin her own married life, the same trunk that Lilian had brought to Dobbs Ferry from Georgetown in 1865. Louisa never acknowledged my letter, which may have been overlooked amid tissue paper wrapping a delicate article of her trousseau and thrown, unopened and unread, into the stove.

I can no longer recollect the words that I'd sensibly arranged on paper. The gist of it? I caught a red-hot ball in the throat from one of Henry Shrapnel's shells, was taken to Harper's Ferry by wagon, and thence to Georgetown aboard a hospital train on the Baltimore and Ohio tracks. I was given a bed in Union Hospital and put into the capable hands of Miss Greenwood, who would become Louisa's mother. Hers were not the hands of a lady who would play "Nearer, My God, to Thee" on a harmonium, but of a woman who could have played "Charlotte the Harlot," by ear on a beat-up

Eden's Clock 43

piano in a miner's camp. Lilian was a bighearted, big-boned woman, "full of pep and pepper," as she liked to say, no man's rag doll and nobody's fool. In over forty years, I seldom got the better of her in an argument. It's hard to get a word in edgewise with a woman who knows her own mind. (Even harder for a fellow who can't get a word out to beat the devil.) She was tough as a three-day-old scone and, when she wanted to be, soft as a pincushion after she'd taken out the pins. When she let down her long brown hair and shook it out the way women do when they've shed their corsets and their modesty, my jaw would drop in admiration. Even when we had gotten on in years, I would sit at the kitchen table, stroking the yellow oilcloth, and watch her fuss over the old Elmira stove. In case Louisa never got my letter, I ought to write her another.

Dear daughter,

Your mother was not wholly one thing or another. She was less than perfect, to be sure, although to my way of thinking, she was less imperfect than most other women and much less so than men. She was subject to—not whims, there was nothing fickle about her—to enthusiasms (a weak word), to passions, then. She was no bluestocking primping in the flattering mirror of self-regard for having a mind open to

44   NORMAN LOCK

progressive ideas. She carried her banner (and her stick) out of the parlor and into the street. Blustering, bullying men didn't scare her, although she would have stopped short at martyrdom of the Christian or the Hindu sort.

The solitude common to the deaf, dumb, and blind is increased by bereavement. In that first month after Lilian's having gone to ground, I indulged in a sorrow sweetened by nostalgia, shared by most every widow and widower. I buried my face in her clothes, ate her quince jelly till I was sick, and let my gaze wander through her favorite books. I was too distracted to read, but, nonetheless, I came away from their pages with an impression of their authors' outrage against men's inhumanity to women. *The Woman's Bible*, published ten years earlier, offended the self-righteous and provoked hostility in men who solemnly intoned Paul's behest to the Corinthians concerning marriage: "The wife hath not power of her own body, but the husband," ignoring the remainder of the verse, "and likewise also the husband hath not power of his own body, but the wife."

In remembrance of her, I polished the cutlery as vigorously as she would have wished. I trimmed the privet hedges, raked the dropped leaves, and "walked abroad," smiling at her use of the old-fashioned

Eden's Clock 45

expression. I'd carry her walking stick until, feeling anger strengthening in me against the villagers, I left it at home, afraid that I'd knock some fellow's brains out for giving me the cold shoulder or the knowing wink.

My habit had been to walk beside Croton Aqueduct, from the river east to the Minturn estate, and return home on Dobbs Ferry's idea of Broadway. After Lilian threw in her lot with the dead, I would turn off Broadway at Storm Street to visit her earthly remains. I'd sit by her stone and eat a chicken sandwich, chased with a bottle of Hudson River beer. She would be the last person to accuse me of disrespect. Had I gone first, she'd have done the same, possessing a thirst and appetite as keen as any man's. Lilian had been uncommonly bold, like the suffragists and the abolitionists before them, whom I got to know through her. She didn't give a hang if she was hooted at, lampooned in the papers, or pelted with cowpats. Nor did she fear imprisonment, although her visitations to Sing Sing gave her a hint of what it meant to be shut up behind brick walls. She was not afraid of death. Like Mrs. Stanton and Miss Anthony, she received her share of anonymous threats on her life. Even a small town has its assassins, Jack. They lurk behind drawn shades, in parlors redolent of lavender and dust, on the porches of general stores, where grumpy men mutter darkly,

46   NORMAN LOCK

and in smoke-filled barrooms, where glances are full of covetousness and murder.

How well I recall the day that President Garfield was shot by Charles Guiteau, a lunatic office seeker, in Washington City: July 2, 1881. One remembers a grim day, while ten thousand ordinary ones are forgotten. The president had planned to travel up the Hudson in his private steam yacht and, after putting in at Taylor's Dock, spend Independence Day being shown the sights of Dobbs Ferry by its wealthiest citizen, Cyrus Field, who got rich laying the transatlantic cable. Lilian had hung the flag from our second-story window and, together with Louisa, wound red-white-and-blue bunting through the hairpin fence. The streets were bright and noisy with patriotic show. Lilian believed that Garfield, a champion of civil rights for Negroes, "might do the cause some good." We joined the throng at the pier and waited for his yacht. Instead of the president, news of an attempt on his life arrived at the telegraph office. He died seventy-nine days later. Garfield paid the toll demanded of him and passed on through the gate, enlarging Death's kingdom by one, as will we all, in our turn—even you, Jack London, who, in the vigor of your early manhood, look as if you might twist Death's arm behind his back until he cries "Uncle!"

On the day of Garfield's funeral in Cleveland, every shop and office, forge and factory in Dobbs

Ferry closed at ten o'clock in the morning. Minute guns began to boom at one. Lilian and I stood outside the "Little White Church" as the bells were rung by the sexton, Joseph King, who had tolled the death of Lincoln sixteen years before. Our Civil War all but officially over and his beloved Union triumphant, that good man allowed himself a night at the theater, where a comedy would be performed that might relax the spring of action and ease his mind of nagging doubt. But the nation's cardinal assassin, Booth, insisted on turning it into a tragedy. Charles Guiteau struck down a president because of his frustrated desire to be our consul in Paris, a madman who spoke not a word of French.

Before the war, I was apprenticed to my father's brother, Harry, who had mustered in at Albany and mustered out near Fort Monroe, Virginia, dead of a bullet to the brain. Discharged from the army, I took over his clockmaker's shop, next to the grammar school on High Street. As I waited for Lilian to join me in Dobbs Ferry, when the war would reach its bitter end, I hired a young man to wait on customers. I felt more at ease keeping my back to them as I poked among the mechanical entrails laid open to my inspection. In those days, customers paid scant attention to my condition. I was not the only man to come home with fewer parts of his anatomy than he had left with. Even in a small place like Dobbs

Ferry, soldiers missing hands, feet, ears, eyes, noses, arms, or legs could be seen sitting on front porches and under the striped awning of Fralinger's hardware. Vocal cords may be no great loss, in comparison, but human intimacy is hampered by their absence, and I felt it keenly.

Time is always fingering the beads of the abacus. As human remnants of that terrible strife grew old or sick, it moved their mortal counters from life to death. In a generation or two, the maimed and mangled became a rarity in Dobbs Ferry. The last of them to leave this life was Percy Bunting, who had been wounded in the Battle of the Wilderness. With such a name, he should have been a poet, instead of a legless man who rode about the village sidewalks on a low four-wheeled cart propelled by hands mittened in shoe leather. Never once did I hear him curse his fate or those who loomed above him, whole and happy and, oftentimes, oblivious of him as they went about the business of the living. His eyes shaded by the brim of his forage cap, he would look up at us and smile— yes, the man smiled, as if he held the green end of the stick and not its muck end. His exertions must have pained him (a foolish understatement). I would not have been so brave.

One morning as I was shaving (how Lilian hated the flecks of dried lather that plastered the mirror above the washstand!), I could not remember the shape of her mouth, which I had kissed, at first eagerly, later fondly, and, at the last—if truth be told—perfunctorily. Had her lips been thin or bowed, moist or chapped? Had she pursed them in thought and bitten them in anger? I can't recollect, yet even now I can smell the violet pastilles she sucked when she dressed putrid wounds at Union Hospital.

6

A month after Death had unkindly stopped for Lilian, I received an envelope mailed from San Francisco by Mr. Herbert Wallace, in charge of the public works of that city. He invited me to inspect the Union Depot and Ferry Building's tower clock to see if I could fix it. My trip west would be paid for by the city, regardless of outcome. I'd been recommended by Arthur Biggs, who had been director of maintenance for White Plains, the Westchester County seat, where, years before, I had restored a clock of identical manufacture, although much inferior in size, to that at the Union Depot.

According to a pamphlet that Wallace enclosed with his letter:

> The Union Depot clock tower rises 235 feet above the Embarcadero and can be seen by passersby all along Market Street,

50   NORMAN LOCK

> San Francisco's main thoroughfare. Mr.
> A. Page Brown, architect, modeled the
> tower on that of the Seville Cathedral.
> Manufactured in Boston, Massachusetts,
> by E. Howard & Company, the clock is
> the largest in the United States. Its face is
> twenty-two feet in diameter. The eleven-
> foot-long minute hand and seven-and-
> one-half-foot hour hand are operated by a
> seven-day mechanism powered by a nine-
> hundred-pound weight.

Wallace had written in the margin, "The hands are so damn big that the clock can gain or lose as much as fifteen minutes in an hour, depending on the direction of the wind. It's my hope that you can regulate its waywardness."

Think of it, Jack! Fifteen minutes lost in a single hour! I wonder if you can appreciate what that inexactitude, magnified by the height of the tower and the diameter of the clock face, means to a clocksmith. It would be as if you were to open a book of yours fresh from the printing press and found that all the commas were missing. Wallace's invitation was a glove flung in my face. I spent the day examining myself: Was I equal to the greatest challenge of my career? The chief of engineering inside the *Amerika* boiler room could not have been more filled with doubt when his ship,

Eden's Clock 51

the world's largest, left Hamburg last month on her maiden voyage.

I was sixty-two; the years were like weights of a pendulum clock at its last *tick, tock*. I had buried my wife and was tired of Dobbs Ferry. Up until that time, I had traveled no farther than Rhinebeck, New York, to wrestle a willful clock into submission. The mechanisms I had taken to pieces and put together again were pygmies compared to San Francisco's behemoth.

I pictured myself high above the Embarcadero, in the Union Depot and Ferry Building tower, like Galileo at his telescope, watching the planets revolve around him, or Captain Nemo, his hand on the controls of the *Nautilus*—only my hand would be on the governor of time. What an extraordinary thing to do and to remember! To pit myself against the strongest current in the universe would expunge the memory of my cowardice in Miller's cornfield, when the Louisiana Tigers rolled over us.

Do I dare? I asked myself.

I know what you'd have said, Jack. But I'm not built like you.

I went next door to ask Henry Kopf what he thought of Mr. Wallace's offer. I doubt that Henry considered me much more than an acquaintance, in spite of our having shared a hedge for twenty years. How could it be otherwise, since he knew nothing of my desires and ambitions or of my declining interest

52 Norman Lock

in either? A personality can't be conveyed by chalk on a slate. We made a fine pair: He spoke as though he had come home from his shoemaker's bench, with a mouth full of nails, and I not at all. Still, he was someone I could palaver with, in a manner of speaking, and after years of playing charades with me, he could interpret my gestures almost as well as Lilian. I never did learn to sign properly, seeing little use in it, unless the town learned likewise.

I've been invited to san francis— The chalk stick broke in two. I took a piece that had fallen in my lap and continued: —co to mend a clock. what do you think?

I waited for Henry to get his thoughts in order. He didn't believe in speaking in haste. To oil the works, he poured each of us a tumbler of whiskey, which the Dutch call "courage." In the army, I had drunk barrels of the stuff to keep my courage up. After my wounding, I drank more, believing that strong drink might splice my severed vocal cords. (The soused have a cunning all their own.) Nothing came of it, except for my near ruin. It doesn't take Jeremiah to foresee the effect of the shakes on a clock's innards. Sitting opposite me at his kitchen table, Kopf appeared to be deep in thought. He fingered his chin, pulled at a pendulous earlobe, put his hand inside his shirt, and scratched. Becoming impatient, I rubbed the chalkboard clean with my sleeve, sending a cloud of dust into the air, which caught Kopf in the back of his throat and set him coughing. He downed two whiskeys in quick succession.

WELL, HENRY?

As wall-eyed as a yellow pickerel, he stared at me a moment before his head came to rest on a plate of sauerbraten.

The next morning, I went to visit Lilian at her grave. I sat on her neighbor's stone, up to my hocks in withered grass. Evidently, Arnold Burrows's next of kin had not seen fit to provide for his plot's perpetual maintenance. My slate resting on my knees like a Ouija board, I waited for Lilian to speak through the chalk. But she kept her thoughts to herself. Mine wandered to the Fox sisters, Leah, Margaretta, and Catherine, famous clairvoyants until, in 1888, Maggie and Kate confessed to being flimflam artists, before a packed audience at the New York Academy of Music. Prior to the revelation of their swindle, Lilian and I, together with Susan B. Anthony, had gone by train to Manhattan to see the Foxes raise the ghost of the prophet Jeremiah, who, ages past, had foretold ruin. Time has borne him out in spades.

Miss Anthony wished to know when women would be enfranchised. We leaned forward expectantly. "Well?" she demanded of Maggie, who had been chosen to mouth the words of the prophet. She replied in a language that a faction of the audience insisted was Aramaic, although an equally noisy opposition maintained that she had spoken gibberish, "on account of delirium tremens." (Maggie was a terrible sot.) P. T. Barnum, down from his Oriental palace in Bridgeport, Connecticut, called for a copper to escort Miss Anthony to the curb. The three Foxes were his protégées, as well as former lodgers at the Barnum Hotel, on Broadway and Maiden Lane. Nearly twenty years have passed, and still we wait for the prophet, Miss Fox, God, or Congress to answer the suffragist's question.

That morning at Dobbs Ferry's graveyard, my question concerning a journey to distant San Francisco also remained unanswered. Mr. Burrows's grass spoke in whispers, although not to me.

7

I locked my front door and walked to Taylor's Dock, my clothes and a few books stuffed into a Gladstone bag. A leather satchel held tools to persuade fractious clocks to mend their ways. To the uninitiated, my trade would appear as mysterious as that of a priest, who, at the sound of a little bell rung by an altar boy, turns wine to blood and bread to flesh. We whose sacred charge is to serve time ring no bells; the clock itself tolls the changes. For us, the heart of the mystery lies in the toothed wheel called the escapement,

Eden's Clock 55

invented, as every horologist knows, by Galileo, who did not live to hear the first *tick, tock*. To have missed the prelude matters not at all, because time itself is soundless and Death is dumb. It falls to men and women to give it voice, one raised in protest, pain, or, for ardent souls, joy.

A commotion on the dock broke the mirror in which I had been reflecting. People were gathered in a knot, their voices raised in a hubbub that woke Gadfrey and his dog, both of whom slept on a pallet in the freight shed. Frank Reynolds, one of the town's chief loafers, was poking at the water with a boat hook.

"What is it?" asked Gadfrey, fingering his goiter.

"Can't tell," replied Reynolds, who liked to drink and saw no reason to deny himself the pleasure.

Consensus waffled as each onlooker put in his two cents.

"Looks like a dead sturgeon."

"Dead dog, maybe."

"Belly's blowed the hell up."

"Ain't a dog, neither."

"Not my dog," said Gadfrey, whom everyone referred to as "the judge," though none could remember why. His mutt was barking and snarling at the sodden bundle in the river.

"Looks like a man, don't it?"

"Pull him in, Frank."

"I'm trying, dammit all!"

"Don't it look like a man?"

"More like a bundle of rags," said Arnie Jacobs, the town barber, who had been the first to spot the item in the water. He was waiting for the Albany boat, in a fragrant atmosphere of bay rum. He cut hair in a narrow shop across the road. When business was slow, he would stand on a packing case, strike a pose like William Jennings Bryan's when railing against the cross of gold, and croak to the disembarking passengers, "Shave and a haircut, two bits."

"It *is* a man—black and bloated!"

"Hook his belt, Frank."

"Wendell, he don't have a belt."

"He's got a piece of rope around his waist. Hook that, why don't you?"

"Hook it yourself!"

"I got on my brand-new Florsheims."

"Piss on your Florsheims!"

"Here he comes."

"Throw a rope around his neck, Johnson."

"I don't got a rope."

"Frank, bring him the hell in!"

"Get ahold of him, man!"

"I got him, I got him."

"It's a colored boy."

"Been in the water a long while, I'd say."

"God Almighty, would you look at his face!"

"Mud crabs have been at him."

Eden's Clock   57

"Ate the eyes out of his head."

"What a shame!"

"It's just a darky, ma'am."

"Must have fallen overboard."

"Pushed, more like it."

"Hell of a thing!"

"The poor so-and-so."

"He don't feel a thing."

"Just a colored boy."

"What do you got there, Frank?" asked Crawford, who had charge over the Dobbs Ferry stop.

"A drowned colored boy."

"Hell of a thing!"

"No shave and a haircut here, Arnie!"

"He's queered my pitch, all right."

"Get that dead shine off my dock! The *Adirondack*'s due in five minutes!"

"Do I look like a spittoon to you, Crawford? You spat an oyster on my shoes."

"You ought to show some respect, Mr. Crawford."

"Wipe your chin!"

"What'll we do with the boy?"

"Put him on a baggage truck."

"I don't want any corpses on my baggage truck!"

"It's just the one, Crawford."

"You and Frank, carry him to the other side of the tracks. Let the Hudson River Railroad deal with it. God Almighty, here comes the boat!"

58   NORMAN LOCK

"Mr. Crawford, you shouldn't take the Lord's name in vain."

"Oh hell, it's only a drowned coon."

I'd seen the like before, washed up on the Union side of the Potomac River. Lilian and I had gone for an airing along the "Grand Old Ditch," as the Chesapeake and Ohio Canal is called. We had walked as far as the Georgetown aqueduct, and turning back, we saw the body of a black man. He was one of many escaped slaves who hoped to free themselves by swimming across the river from Virginia. He was dressed the same as the Negro who was being roughly handled by Frank Reynolds and a commercial traveler wearing a fancy vest.

I crossed the tracks and looked at the body, which had been laid on the doorstep of a toolshed belonging to the railroad. I could do nothing for him. Everything that could be done to him had been done. He had been rendered into meat by time and the elements. I could only hope that the brutes who saw him as a thing had not beaten and mortified him into what is less than human while he lived. If there are bootblacks in heaven, he'll spend his life to come leaning over shoes as the blessed angels sit and smoke cigars.

Was I indignant at this latest instance of the same old story, Jack, one older than Egypt? Yes, but how rage, how speak my mind with a pencil or a stick of

Eden's Clock 59

chalk? I turned away. The westering sun struck the shining rails and made my sight go black.

8

I went aboard the *Adirondack*, bound for the Battery, at the end of Manhattan, where the Hudson River empties into Upper New York Bay. I joined a score of Chinese men on the passenger deck, returning from an Indian summer picnic on Iona Island. Accompanying them were several ladies who had taught them to read at a missionary Sunday school. The men took a pragmatic interest in English, though not in the Gospels, whose promises to the poor and meek were small comfort to them, particularly after the Chinese Exclusion Act of 1882 increased their misery by barring women from the Orient. All year, the men had put aside a portion of their coolie wages earned in steam laundries, whose heat and hiss, thump and roar might have come from the vents of hell.

On the boat, they kept to themselves. Leaning on the railings, they smoked cigarettes and let their gazes rest on the unfolding scenery. Their clothes smelled of gunpowder, a residue of the fireworks they had set off on the island. A few young men flew dragon kites. Several older ones, dressed in black tunics and round hats, played Chinese music, which the white passengers, who had boarded at Cortlandt

60   NORMAN LOCK

and Croton-on-Hudson, mocked by playing on their combs. Ignorant, they'd have pinched their nostrils shut in disgust at the music of *The Magic Flute*, but called for encores of Spencer and Ossman singing "Crappy Dan." You know the sort, Jack.

I was captivated by the strangeness of the scene, as I would have been by a scarlet ibis from Egypt in Central Park, a paradise fish from the Pearl River Basin in Croydon Reservoir, or a woman wearing a fox stole and "flowerpot hat" in Bandit's Roost. Even so, the men behaved every bit as well as any white Christians would have done. No one smoked opium from a long pipe, roasted a dog on deck, or burned joss sticks to a heathen god. I witnessed not a single instance of the "licentious mixing" of men and women of different races that has been claimed by ministers fulminating from pulpits, backbiting citizens in parlors, and two-faced politicians stumping against the "yellow peril." Never would I believe that a female missionary had gone "in the shrubbery with her favorite Sunday school scholar," as had been reported in a summer number of the *Illustrated Police News*. Intimacy on board the ferryboat went no further than a missionary's wave of the hand to one of her students and a friendly word spoken in his native tongue.

A man who had boarded at Croton sat beside me. To discourage him, I gave my attention to a pair of side-wheelers making for opposite destinations, like

Eden's Clock   61

contrary Jesus bugs. He lit a cigar and, letting the smoke drift where it pleased, cleared his throat, a sound I recognized as the prelude to a conversation.

"McGlinn's the name," he said. "Supplier of paper to the printing trade."

I opened your book *The People of the Abyss*. Lilian had pressed a red peony between its pages, as another woman might have marked a favorite poem in *Sonnets from the Portuguese*. To be honest, Jack, I'd mistaken the book for one of your adventure yarns; I'd never have brought it along with me otherwise. McGlinn studied his stogy while I read the passage on which my gaze had fallen:

> There were seven rooms in this abomination called a house. In six of the rooms, twenty-odd people, of both sexes and all ages, cooked, ate, slept, and worked. In size the rooms averaged eight feet by eight, or possibly nine. The seventh room we entered. It was the den in which five men "sweated." It was seven feet wide by eight long, and the table at which the work was performed took up the major portion of the space. On this table were five lasts, and there was barely room for the men to stand to their work, for the rest of the space was heaped with cardboard, leather, bundles of shoe uppers,

and a miscellaneous assortment of materials used in attaching the uppers of shoes to their soles.

Your tour of the lower depths of Whitechapel was an eye-opener, Jack. You would have seen the same on the Lower East Side, which is more crowded with the down-and-out than any other city in the world, not excepting Shanghai and Bombay.

"Can't say I care for Chinamen," said McGlinn, slumping on the bench.

I sank deeper into the heaving sea of print on my lap.

"Cat got your tongue?" He hated silence, I saw at once, and would talk until he croaked.

I kept my eyes on the page, though the words were like flying fish fleeing from a whale.

Annoyed, he huffed, spat, and tossed his stogy overboard.

Let him stew, I told myself. It would be a waste of chalk or lead to speak to him.

He was one of those people who can't stand to be stoppered. Like an agitated bottle of soda pop, they will fizz over as soon as they're uncorked. What bubbled up in him was hatred for "the yellow heathens staining the white Christian roots of our great democracy."

"A Chink stinks to high heaven! No wonder,

considering that chop suey they swill. I ate it once in Albany, during a convention of paper merchants."

Feather merchants, more likely.

"Disgusting stuff, wouldn't feed it to a dog. I did the 'green apple quickstep' that night, you bet!"

And you, fat man, stink of cigars, unwashed clothes, and raw onions.

"Turns them yellow, I shouldn't wonder."

I'd have something to say about your yellow shoes and purple vest, if I were in the mood to scribble.

"I'd hang myself if I was one of them, by God I would!

I'd knot the noose, by God I would!

"I don't understand these Sunday school biddies. Course they're plain as sin. Just look at those scrawny hens! Can't get a man 'less he's got a pigtail down his back and smells of joss. I've no beef with kraut eaters, or Polacks, or even dagos. I buy my panatelas from a spic cigar roller and get my shoes shined by a colored boy. But I draw the line at the Chinese. We should cut off their pigtails and their pricks and send them back to the Celestial Empire, C.O.D."

He treated me to a song popular with the Anti-Chinese League:

John Chinaman, John Chinaman
But five short years ago,
I welcomed you from Canton, John,

But I wish I hadn't though;

I imagined that the truth, John,
You'd speak when under oath,
But I find you'll lie and steal too—
Yes, John, you're up to both.

Out of breath, if not of opinions, McGlinn wheezed to a stop. I could see that he was pleased with himself and that he expected me to break my silence or, at least, give him a wink and a nod of approval. I regarded him as I would have if presented with one of nature's gross mistakes, which would have been better for the human race had it been aborted or annulled.

"It's like talking to a post," he said, wiping his perspiring face with a handkerchief of doubtful lineage. "I never met a dumber son of a bitch!"

I remembered Lilian, how she would not hold her tongue in the presence of ignoramuses. She would give them a piece of her mind. She was scared of no one and would spare no one her indignation, not even a brute who beat his wife to show her who was boss. She could cut a man to the bone with her sharp tongue. She could roast him in the fire of her kindled rage.

I raised my middle finger, an eloquent gesture of contempt made famous by "Old Hoss" Radbourn, pitcher for the Boston Beaneaters, on opening day '86. I could've filled a dozen slates with reasons why the

greasy lump sitting next to me, stuffed into a check-
ered suit, was a jackass, but I wouldn't have driven
the point home with one clean swing. His expression changed from smug self-righteousness to that of
a man whose noggin had been split by a baseball bat.
And then the bile and the venom rushed out of his
mouth, as if I'd spooned ipecac down his throat.

"I'll be damned—"

The devil is welcome to you.

"—if you ain't a Chink-lovin' Red! I wish we'd had
you in Wyoming, at Rock Springs, when the Knights
of Labor—hardworking Finns, Swedes, Welshmen,
and Germans—ousted the yellow weasels willing to
work for a wage no human being, leastways no white
human being, could live on. It's debatable whether
the Chinese are human. Some say yes, some say no.
I say they're on par with the monkeys they resemble.
Let 'em put on their little round hats and hop for wop
organ grinders. The Tacoma method is the only way
to handle their kind. Round them up, stick them on
a train, and ship them to the next town. Keep them
moving up the line. Folks had the right idea at Rock
Springs: If they won't go peaceably, shoot the yellow fuckers, hang them from the gutter spouts, scalp
them, torch their shacks, and throw them into the
fire, dead or alive. The Almighty has a heathen hell
for them, with Chink devils to stuff them full of chop
suey and lychee nuts till they choke."

66   NORMAN LOCK

I fingered the chalk in my pocket as if it were a stick of dynamite. But I'd learned that the surest way to get somebody's goat was to say nothing.

"Swine!" he shouted, giving me a push as he rose from the bench, which sent me flying into the midst of half a dozen missionaries. Gulls like strong rowers passed overhead, shouting *excelsior* in the hoarse language of scavenger birds.

The young men let go their kite strings and helped the ladies to their feet. The commotion had left their clothing in disarray. Embarrassed, they fixed their skirts and blushed in the shadow of their straw bonnets. McGlinn proceeded to lambaste white missionary women "who hide their unnatural desires behind a lot of Bible-thumping."

The infuriated Chinese had their blood up. They would have seized McGlinn and thrown him overboard if a blast of the boat's steam whistle had not put an end to the Boxer Rebellion on the Hudson.

"I don't allow hell-raising on board the *Adirondack*!" bellowed the red-faced captain from the pilothouse. "I'll put you idiots ashore at the next mudflat if you don't settle down." Amplified by a megaphone, his voice filled the hollows of my chest. In such a voice, God will pass sentence on His botched creation.

McGlinn, sample case in tow, went off in a huff to the steamer's saloon, where he could get a sausage

Eden's Clock 67

and a glass of beer to rid his mouth of the taste of humiliation.

I went down onto the main deck and leaned against the jack staff in the bow. The Stars and Stripes beat in the evening wind, which carried the smell of dead things in the mud exposed by the retreating tide.

Our destiny, they tell us, is to pull the savages from the muck of history's fetid, fever-ridden back-waters. At the New-York Historical Society, I saw the five allegorical paintings of Thomas Cole's *The Course of Empire*, showing the advance from savagery to arcadia and then—exhausted and corrupt—the steep slide backward to destruction and desolation, represented by a solitary Corinthian column presiding over ruins.

The *Adirondack* steamed past the Elysium Fields at Hoboken, where the blessed eat hot dogs and the gods wear cleats. Her side wheels churned the dark water into froth. Her blunt bow made waves that spread shoreward and slipped up the tarred pilings at the Manhattan Iron Works, the Erie Railroad oil depot, the Delaware and Hudson Canal coal yard. They thrust their dirty fingers into the river, called *Ca-ho-ha-ta-te-a* by the Iroquois and *Muh-he-kun-ne-tuk* (the river that flows two ways) by the Mohicans. How prosaic *Hudson* sounds in comparison, how lacking in majesty!

68   NORMAN LOCK

The roof of Castle Garden turned gold, before giving up its luster to the coming of the night.

9

The *Adirondack* bumped against the dock. The dark river, its roiling surface oiled by careless factories along the Hudson, slipped up to her gunwales, then subsided with a slap against the hull. Night had fallen over the Battery and its wooden teeth of piers. Hills outlined by lights, Staten Island might have been an immense black ship moored in the Upper Bay. Having set our hats and clothes to rights and gathered our grips and cases, we made our way to the lower deck and filed out of the boat by the landing stage. No sooner had our feet touched ground than a squad of policemen from the First Precinct station encircled the Chinese, missionaries, and me. Wielding sticks, they prodded us into an empty shed. A Chinese student, taking exception to a poke in his ribs, wrested the truncheon from a copper's grip. Instantly, he was set upon by a scrum of burly men, who, as guardians of law and order, taught the Chink a civics lesson. He sank to his knees as if giving thanks to the land of the free; then he lay down and, despite the encouragement of a polished boot, would not get up again. The missionaries attacked with umbrellas. Experienced in subduing suffragists, the cops trussed them up in their own voluminous skirts.

Those who could walk to a nearby warehouse, where we could be "sorted out," did so, helped by a stick in the back or a yank on a queue. Those who couldn't walk were carried at the public's expense. Not even Susan B. Anthony could have objected to unequal treatment of the sexes; the ladies were man-handled just like the men.

"There must be some mistake!" shouted one of the missionaries, who had every right to uncorset her Sunday school demeanor and give way to an unlady-like rage. "Unless the world's gone mad."

Clockmakers banish chance and accident from timepieces, although not from the wider world, where derangement reigns. I expect the same holds true for storytellers, eh, Jack?

"You Chinamen are under arrest for the murder of Sally Root of Bayard Street, who was found in a trunk at a Chink flophouse on Mott Street, next door to the mission," said a roly-poly captain topped by a tall helmet, whose leather strap snuggled between his double chins.

"Nonsense!" cried the ladies in unison.

"Until we've caught the Chinaman responsible for this atrocity, this lot of Celestials is all guilty. I'm taking in you old battleaxes for aiding and abetting."

"What rubbish!"

70 NORMAN LOCK

One hand plucking the captain's sleeve, the other holding a sausage, McGlinn swore that I had furnished the fireworks that the Chinese set off on Iona Island, in rehearsal for dynamiting the stock exchange. "He's a bolshie anarchist on his way to meet 'Red' Emma Goldman!"

Lacking the means to defend myself from slander, I was at the copper's mercy, which McGlinn had squeezed dry with a "fin" slipped into his greasy palm.

"And you, mister, are under suspicion," said the captain, pointing a stubby finger at me. He would have read the bafflement on my face, for he went on to say, "Of conspiring to commit destruction of private property, arson, mayhem, and murder."

The world's mainspring had snapped. But who could hear the shouts of a mute?

I was pushed into a van already packed with conspirators. The Chinese were silent, as befits the terrified, although their teeth rattled when the meat wagon jolted over cobblestones. We were taken to City Prison, Tammany Hall's million-dollar hornswoggle, which the wags of Newspaper Row dubbed "the Tombs" because of its resemblance to an Egyptian mausoleum. Before I could admire its turret clock, a bullock of a cop shoved me through the prison door.

I was put in a cell with two Chinese students. Mistaking me for a deaf-mute, they forsook English and gabbled in their native tongue. That night I wondered if, like Dantès, the Count of Monte Cristo, I would wear away in this Château d'If, connected to the Manhattan Criminal Courts building by a covered walkway high above Franklin Street, called "the Bridge of Sighs."

10

Every so often, we were taken into the prison yard and made to walk in a circle. I stared at the back of the man in front of me, always the same man, until I could have told you the number of hairs on his head. I became self-conscious as I wondered whether the man behind me was giving the back of my neck the same fierce scrutiny. Soon enough, I became entangled with the man in front of me, so that the man following me stumbled and fell, breaking the circle. The guard "gave me some stick." The next time it happened, I was taken from the yard and denied further airings.

I was awakened by a groan from one of my Chinese companions, signifying pain in the universal language of the sick at heart. I beat the tin cup provided for our common thirst against the bars. A jailer unlocked the iron door, which groaned on its hinges, in sympathy,

72   NORMAN LOCK

perhaps, with those within who might be innocent, if unlucky. Who can say whether Cassius got it wrong when he told Brutus that the fault is not in our stars, but in ourselves? The jailer twisted my arm until I, too, groaned, as though he were a professor of anatomy demonstrating the limit of the elbow joint. He stopped short of its dislocation. His eyes asked the Chinese cowering by the plastered wall whether they had understood the lesson and was gratified to see that they had. He dragged me from the cell and down three flights of stairs, the keys on his belt making a manic music. He put me in solitary confinement to reflect on my sins.

"One thing I hate worse than a Chinaman is an anarchist," he said as he closed the door. "As far as I'm concerned, you can rot!" he snarled as he locked it.

I am to become Edmond Dantès after all, I said to myself bitterly. But I could expect no Abbé Faria to dig a tunnel with a spoon, by which we both could escape our common end. Time, having turned anarchic, seemed bent on my destruction. During the havoc on the wharf, I'd been struck on the mouth. Whether by a policeman or a flailing Sunday school student, I couldn't have said. One of my teeth had been broken. I felt as if the several aspects of myself no longer meshed as they should have. The machinery of time had also lost a tooth: What had been

Eden's Clock   73

regular became wayward. No longer rigorous, it was elastic, like dough before its shape is set in the oven.

As I lay on a cot stained by its previous occupants, I recalled having caught the scent of coffee inside the warehouse shed where we'd been penned. Burlap sacks of beans may well have been loaded onto a packet and shipped upriver to Latimore's grocery store the week before the roundup on the pier. Why, I may have roasted, ground, and brewed a portion of those beans in my kitchen! In that narrow place, I scoffed at what Prince Hamlet had said about the nutshell and at Thoreau's words in praise of solitude. Hamlet was mad, after all, and Thoreau's mind had likely been unhinged by the Concord Transcendentalists.

A place where nothing happens is a clocksmith's hell, and so the Tombs turned out to be for me, whose attempt to tick off the passing days, in the approved manner of the imprisoned, was soon frustrated by the absence of sunlight in my cell and the sameness of the cuisine. In short order, I became lost to time and would have likely graduated from City Prison to Bloomingdale Asylum had it not been for the Bible given to me by a do-gooder from the missionary society. Under the circumstances, Trow's *General Directory of the Boroughs of Manhattan and Bronx* would

74   NORMAN LOCK

have made me rapturous. A book, after all, is like a
piece of clockwork; both show a world up close and in
miniature. The Bible is packed with rip-roaring yarns.
The Lord's wrath against the bloody city and the sev-
enty years' desolation prophesied by Ezekiel and Jeremiah are as thrilling as *The Sea-Wolf* and *The Call of the
Wild*. I identified with Job, as well as with Humphrey
Van Weyden and John Thornton, who matched wits
with the elements, as I had done with time, which I
tried to tame.

Shut up in the Tombs, I soon realized how small
a man I am. I'm not of the same stuff as your men of
iron will nor of the Bible's grandees. I was not Job
or your old Indian man Imber, who came to Daw-
son City seeking the Law, only to be crushed by it. I
was Fred Heigold, a village clocksmith. I longed for
unremarkable Dobbs Ferry, the air and light of the
place, and for the river that moved at two knots an
hour, the speed of a mountain of cloud slowly tearing and mending in one of summer's breezes blowing
too high to shake the aspen leaves. I never left my
cell, except to carry the waste bucket to the privy. My
meals came down on a tin plate, which I ate with
my hands. Without a slate or paper, I couldn't make
myself heard. The jailers jeered at my clumsy attempts
at pantomime.

"Will you look at him scratch!"

"He's got lice."

Eden's Clock 75

"And bugs."

"Terrible lot of bedbugs this time of year."

"A regular army of vermin."

"It stinks in here. Why don't you give him a wash?"

"I'm afraid to get too close."

"Well, unless he's got a stick of dynamite stuck up his ass, what're you afraid of?"

One day, a tramp was cast up like Jonah into my cell, which, except for me, had been empty since the start of my quarantine for infectious anarchism. Finding it balmier than an alley or a subway entrance, he stripped himself of insulating layers of newsprint worn beneath his shreds and tatters. "Would you like something to read?" he asked drolly.

I gave him to understand that I would. Sated by Bible stories, I was eager for news of twentieth-century shenanigans. He presented me with an October number of *The Sun*, in whose breezy accounts of metropolitan life could be seen the persistence of human folly and distress.

HERE'S A NEW BRAND OF SPOOKS.

G. Washington and M. Aurelius Are Members of It.

A crowd of spiritualists were sitting about a fireside in Mount Vernon on a rainy Sunday afternoon last spring talking over the great mysteries of the world, especially those of ancient Egypt. Four or five of them were merely believers, but George Plummer and Mrs. Florence Stegman were fully developed mediums.

Suddenly Mr. Plummer, who is a trance medium, began to go under control. At the same moment, Mrs. Stegman, a clairvoyant and clairaudient, began to have impressions. It was an Egyptian named Nebsini, a person dead some 10,000 years who had control of Mr. Plummer. The spirits who flitted into the clairvoyant vision of Mrs. Stegman were also Egyptians, mainly priests and . . .

JEWS APPEAL TO ROOSEVELT.

Five hundred Jews crowded into the Sixty-ninth Street tabernacle last night and sat for nearly three hours, while rabbis and laymen poured forth the story of the Odessa and Kiev massacres. They listened with patient and intense faces until the Rev. Dr. Pikus, breaking into the high chant of the Jews, pictured in Yiddish the crimes of the last three days. His audience burst into tears; men and children and the sprinkling of women in the balcony lost control of themselves, covered their faces with their hands and sobbed. . . .

COULDN'T FEED ONE MORE.

Mother of Six Cut Her Own Throat.

Mrs. Annie White, 43 years old, of 110 Seventh Avenue, was a prisoner in the West Side Court yesterday, charged with attempted suicide. She is the mother of six children with whom she lives in three tiny rooms. . . .

PENITENT WITH PAVING STONE.

Whatever may have been the pangs of conscience suffered by James Lynch, a laborer of 20 Bowery, they were quickly dispelled and as quickly replaced by feelings of wrath at his experiences at the Salvation Army barracks at 18 East Broadway. Lynch entered the barracks at 10:30 o'clock Saturday night and said he was looking for salvation and wanted to reform.

He found himself lying in the gutter after being propelled in record time from the barracks. In a moment, Lynch was filled with wrath and called the Salvationists a bunch of lobsters, and then did a little weight-throwing with a paving stone. Lynch was arrested and sent to the Tombs. . . .

Had James Lynch been one of the convicts with whom I was made to march in a circle around the prison yard? He may have been the man I tripped over when I became transfixed by the sight of the back of his neck, unless he was the man behind me whose stare I had felt on the back of my own.

One morning, the prison chaplain stopped to give me the comforts of his Savior. He would have considered me a poor candidate for salvation, since I would neither pray for forgiveness nor confess my sins. Embarrassed, he put a pamphlet warning against "drabs and slatterns" on my pillow and left my cell, never to visit

Eden's Clock   79

again. Since he was a young man, likely fresh from the seminary and inexperienced in the variety of men, I forgave him his innocence.

Christmas Eve would have passed unnoticed, if not for a visit from my jailor, who stopped awhile to share a bottle of rye whiskey and a mince pie "baked by the missus." His mood was a mixture of jollity and weepy sentiment, this man who had never shown me kindness. At the end of his visit, after we had eaten pie and drunk toasts to each other's health (I, too, had grown maudlin), he breathed his spicy breath into my face and, holding my head in his hands, kissed me on both cheeks. "Freddie, dear," he said, "I wish you Merry Christmas. From now on, I will treat you like a brother."

I knew that, in the morning, he would not remember his promise.

The Tombs was cold, my blanket thin, the diet unnourishing. Always liable to fever, I came down with one. The prison surgeon laid a blue pill on my tongue and set a bucket of snow at my bedside. A man walked to his death. I didn't see him go. I heard the groan of the door moving heavily on its hinges, a jangle of keys, the complaint of the door as it slammed shut in the iron jamb—a sound that made me shudder, as the

80   NORMAN LOCK

last Bourbon king would have done in his cell, to hear the blade of the guillotine in the yard strike home.

You know how it is, Jack. In your hoboing days, you did time in the Erie County pen for watching the sunrise over Niagara Falls with no money in your pocket. Time, the juggernaut, taught you that not even a rugged character like you can take what a gang of bullies and brutes dishes out. They didn't break your spirit, not in thirty days. But you learned that a cornered rat is easily stoned, but in a pack, it is formidable, a cog in a clockwork of teeth whose single purpose is to destroy the common enemy, man.

11

On the last morning of 1905, I was taken to the warden's office. He was sitting at a desk of the utilitarian sort often seen with a clerk or a factory manager behind it. A stack of pasteboard files lay next to an ink-stained blotter. If I were to open one, would I find a paper facsimile of myself? It would need to be abridged and biased, as the appraisal of another's soul must be. I wondered if the file contained a letter from Henry Kopf attesting to my good character or one from the Reverend Hardy asserting the opposite. In another written on official stationery, Herbert Wallace may have begged for my release, so that the famous San Francisco clock could resume its useful

Eden's Clock 81

purpose. (Or perhaps Clay, the embalmer, had forwarded to the Tombs an additional bill for "extras.")

"Heigold."

I stood at attention, as once I had done before Lieutenant Colonel Bragg on Smoketown Road, in Maryland.

"You're a clocksmith by trade."

I confirmed the truth of it with a nod of my head.

"I'm fond of that piece." He pointed to a round wall clock flanked by framed photographs of President Theodore Roosevelt and of New York City mayor George B. McClellan, Jr., whose father's unglorified dithering on the battlefield had cost the Union army dearly. Baird Company clocks carried advertisements printed on their papier-mâché faces. Manufactured in Plattsburg, New York, the warden's touted Molliscorium, a liniment produced by Vanner & Prest's.

I know Baird clocks; their machinery is straightforward and honest. This clock had been caught in a seizure, so to speak, which stopped its hands at twelve minutes past three. Whether day or night, only time, in its omniscience, could tell. How frail are our instruments where titanic forces are concerned—none more so than time, which laid waste to the mastodon and wears away mountains! I gazed at the clock face, where an infinite past and an infinite future intersected. No amount of Molliscorium can ease the ache of existence. You know that better than anyone, Jack.

"Can you fix it?" There was, in the warden's voice, something like an itch wanting to be scratched. "It belonged to my father. I'd hate to start the New Year without its familiar ticking."

I NEED MY TOOLS.

He pointed to my gripsack squatting on a chair. It looked forlorn.

IF IT CAN BE FIXED, I WILL FIX IT.

"I admire a man who talks a good game." The warden had been digging underneath his fingernails with a paper knife. "Heigold, your profession is against you, as much as your prior association with that old battleax Susan B. Anthony and your present 'relations' with anarchist Emma Goldman."

I rearranged the features of my face to indicate bewilderment.

He put down the knife. "Who knows better than a clocksmith how to make a time bomb? Last year, the Turks attempted to blow the Ottoman sultan to kingdom come with one, and don't forget the dynamite-mad Fenians." He picked up the knife again and ran a finger over the blunt edge. "You're not one of them, are you?" Pursing his lips, he scrutinized me as intensely as a cat does a mouse before pouncing. He put the knife away in a desk drawer. "No, I think not. I think you're a man with no bone to pick."

A push of an annunciator button was answered by a prisoner wheeling a trolley into the warden's office, accompanied by the odor of roast meat, which made my stomach whinge. "You can pick these bones to your heart's content. Consider it a New Year's Eve treat, Heigold. Let's hope you can get my old man's clock to turn over."

Although I was aware that so abrupt a change in diet would be unwise, I chose to risk the quick step; I reduced the turkey to its parts.

"Well, well, Heigold! Anyone would have thought you were starving!"

What good would it have done to tell him that I was?

"Tell me, Frederick: Do you happen to know anyone whose political temper is, shall we say, hot? I expect that many good people with strong opinions visited your late wife in Dobbs Ferry. People—innocent of any criminal intent—who believed that the world, as perfect as the Almighty has made it, could somehow be made more so. I'd like to sit down and talk to them, man-to-man, to see if we might reach an understanding. My jailhouse is full, Fred; I don't need their business."

Fortunately, I had my supper before he had his answer, which was no. He sighed, as all we mortals do in our helplessness to understand our fellows. He summoned the inmate to take away the trolley. The man looked hungry, and I regretted not having left

84   NORMAN LOCK

him some meat on the bones. Oh, well, he can suck the marrow.

The Baird needed only to be cleaned and oiled to set it going again. A bit of grit can stop a clock, but not time, which will outlive God.

12

Twelve weeks after my arrival at the Tombs, I was taken into a room of gray tiles and cement and scrubbed with red carbolic soap. The water roared from the hose with enough force to bark me to the bone, while the stiff bristles of a long-handled brush stung my mortified flesh. I was handed a towel rough as burlap and, after having dried myself, set down roughly in a chair for the prison barber to do his work. I hurried into my old clothes, which smelled of naphthalene, and was led across the Bridge of Sighs to a municipal courtroom, where a large woman dressed in mourning stood before a scrawny judge, whose black robe made me shudder.

Will they hang me from the clock tower or, perhaps, electrocute me, as they did to ax murderer William Kemmler at Auburn Prison, a method of execution suitable for elephants, as proved on Topsy at Luna Park by Thomas Edison, who burned the poor beast from the inside out and filmed her as she went about her dying? Lacking the stomach for such

Eden's Clock   85

spectacles, I didn't go with Lilian to the Manhattan Vitascope to raise a ruckus on behalf of circus animals, although I had seen there *Admiral Dewey Leading the Land Parade* and *The Wreck of the Battleship Maine*, both filmed by Edison, whom I hate for Topsy's sake.

"Frederick Heigold!" intoned the judge funereally.

I made a face I hoped that the judge would interpret as the look of a grateful guest of the city of New York, which had treated him kindly. I was not feeling well. The courtroom seemed to spin like Sir Hiram Maxim's Captive Flying Machine attraction at Coney Island.

He gestured that I should approach. "Mr. Heigold." He slid a pencil and paper across the polished bench, so that I might answer for myself, a lawyer being conspicuously absent. "Your case has been examined, and no evidence has been found against you."

AM I FREE TO GO? I wrote.

"I can't find you guilty, nor can I exonerate you," he said, ignoring my question. "I can't apologize on behalf of the city of New York, nor can I hold you blameless for getting yourself detained. Justice has not miscarried, Mr. Heigold, because your case has not been tried. Since no decision has been rendered, I have nothing to overturn. My hands are tied." He wiped them on his judicial robe, as a child might after eating a jelly doughnut. "Mr. Heigold, I bear you no ill will, although you have been here under false pretenses and at no little expense to the people of New York." He smiled, then snapped his mouth shut like a frog's on a fly. "Recovering the cost to feed and lodge you for the past ten weeks has been left to my discretion. At the behest of the 'Tombs Angel,' as she's known"—he nodded to the woman in black—"the city will foot the bill for your room and board; moreover, it'll pay for your shave and haircut. I think that's mighty white of our city fathers, don't you agree?"

I WAS WRONGLY ACCUSED!

"Tut-tut!"

WHAT ABOUT THE MAN ON THE BOAT WHO SLANDERED ME?

"We could find no trace of him, a fact—the court must consider facts and only facts—that can only mean he does not now nor did he ever exist."

The Tombs Angel's black shadow fell on the judge's bench, as another had once done on the rooftops of Egypt.

The judge, whose name I hadn't caught, coughed judicially, blew his nose, and leaned toward me. "Do you have anything to say before your case is closed?" Giving me a wink, he said, "As a Freemason and an Odd Fellow, I promise never to reopen it."

WHERE ARE MY CLOTHES, MY BOOKS & TOOLS?

"Because they're not mentioned in your file, I must assume that they, too, never existed. Sometimes, Mr. Heigold, when the watch spring of the mind relaxes,

Eden's Clock 87

fancies steal upon it unawares. I'm told such is the case for those who attend an ether party or go on a bender."

I FIXED THE WARDEN'S CLOCK WITH THEM.

"In exchange for a New Year's Eve dinner, for which misappropriation of prison funds he has been duly censured."

A POLICEMAN TOOK MY WALLET!

"You may have lost it aboard the *Adirondack*. The Hudson River steamers are frequented by pickpockets from Albany. We don't allow them in our borough. Do you have any plans, Mr. Heigold? The city of New York has no further interest in you, but curiosity, even in a judge, is human."

I WAS ON MY WAY TO SAN FRANCISCO.

"Excellent choice! May you be happy in the Paris of the West. Babylon on the Hudson wishes you a pleasant journey. Here's a cigar to smoke on the way."

I DON'T HAVE A TICKET & ALL MY MONEY WAS IN MY WALLET!

"The city is heartless. Delicate matters requiring sympathy or financial assistance are the concern of philanthropists and do-gooders, like Mrs. Rebecca Salome Foster." He gestured in the Tombs Angel's direction. She kept her eyes on me, and I knew better than to flinch under her gaze. The judge stood, gave his robes a tug, ran his fingers through his scant hair, and hurried off to a lodge function. The heavy door

88   NORMAN LOCK

closed soundlessly behind him, leaving Mrs. Foster and me alone in the gloomy chamber.

"Have you eaten today, Mr. Heigold?" she asked.

Like a spaniel shaking water from its ears, I gave her to understand that I had not.

She hung her umbrella on one wrist and, with her other arm, took mine. "I'm sure you won't say no to a chop and a beer."

13

I allowed myself to be taken in hand by this formidable angel, who would have wrestled Jacob to a standstill. As we walked down Centre Street, the pavement heaved, and the automobile horns on Park Row cut me to the quick. Twice, Mrs. Foster was obliged to steady me.

I would learn her history from Robert Winter, to whom she would introduce me. Born in Alabama to a family of wealthy planters, Rebecca Salome Elliott married, in 1865, John Armstrong Foster, a New York City lawyer, who would shortly become a lieutenant colonel in the 175th New York Infantry. Later, he discovered a new vocation in the bottle, to which he paid the closest attention. In 1888, he abandoned Rebecca and their two daughters. She went into perpetual mourning, as if to rehearse her widowhood, which arrived in 1890. She gave herself entirely to the cause

Eden's Clock   89

of prison reform and to the men and women shut up in the Tombs, for whom she was indeed an angel, though one dressed in black.

Sitting opposite her in Farrish's Chop House, at the corner of William and John Streets, I inquired, DID YOU KNOW MY LATE WIFE, LILIAN HEIGOLD?

She leaned forward, her face as I had pictured Martha's, Lazarus's sister, and planted a blessing on my forehead. If not for her peach basket hat and the pork chops on our plates, the scene could have been biblical.

Embarrassed, I looked away, letting my eyes wander over a garish lithograph advertising the Barnum and Bailey Circus till they rested on a clock face above the cashier's cage, an 1886 Ansonia, manufactured in Brooklyn. To my amazement, its hands were sweeping backward in defiance of the law of time. I checked my watch, only to find that it was broken.

"Yes, indeed, I knew Lilian. She did much good at Sing Sing."

My head began to swim. My eyes rolled upward, and all went black.

"Are you all right, Fred?" asked the angel by my side. She was wiping mashed potatoes from my chin with a table napkin. I looked at the clock on the wall; its hands were moving with the current of time, instead of against it. I breathed in relief, nodded to

Mrs. Foster, apologized mutely to the other diners, and took a swig of beer.

"You're as pale as a ghost."

With a fork, I wrote on the oilcloth covering the table: FORGIVE ME.

"There is nothing to forgive. You need a good night's sleep. Now finish your meal, and I'll take you home. I'll feed you up; you look half starved from your ordeal. The Lord has work for you to do, Frederick Heigold. I'm sure of it now that I know you were married to Lilian, my good comrade against men who make war on women, children, and their weaker brethren."

A wet snow fell as we walked between tall brownstones toward Park Avenue. My clothes were those I'd worn in late October, when I left Dobbs Ferry. Snow was falling on my head and down my neck. The Tombs Angel opened her umbrella over me.

"You'll need warm clothing, Mr. Heigold, if you're to go on from here."

Why should I want to go on when I can just as easily turn back?

"Because you have been too long enmeshed in time to go contrary to its direction, which is forward," replied a voice I did not recognize. "As if the sun could do an about-face, rising in the evening and setting at the crack of dawn."

14

I had no time to take stock of Mrs. Foster's apartment. I fell asleep at once in a bedroom kept for her daughters' visits.

A woman is sitting in a chair beside the bed.

"Lilian," I say, pleased to have recovered the use of my voice box. "Lilian," I repeat, touching my throat to feel the vibrations on my fingertips.

"Hello, Fred. You've been running yourself ragged, I hear."

"I've missed you. How've you been keeping?"

"Neat as wax."

She begins to lose her color. I wrinkle my nose at an unpleasantly sweet odor.

"Lilian, you're not yourself." I watch as she turns pale and ashen.

Lucius Clay comes into the room with a tumbler of blue liquid and gives it to Lilian to drink. "We swear by Durfee Fluid for keeping our corpses looking fresh."

I awoke and found my host deadheading purple irises in the "conservatory," as she called a room mobbed with flowers, overlooking Park Avenue and warmed by the morning sun.

"You're finally awake, I see."

HOW LONG WAS I ASLEEP?

"A day and a half."

I would have looked like Lazarus blinking in the sunlight of ancient Bethany, after the darkness of the sepulcher.

"You were feverish. You seemed as though you were wrestling with an angel." She smiled amiably. "I hope it wasn't me."

I HAD A DREAM.

"Would you care to tell me it?"

I shook my head no.

"Quite right. Dreams are nobody's business." She treated me to another piercing gaze; this time it wasn't my character she assayed, but my physique, which is of medium height and build. "Your shape is similar to my husband's. If you don't mind wearing a dead man's clothes, which were fashionable in the '80s, you can help yourself. You'll be the Rip Van Winkle of Park Avenue. Little boys will throw stones at you. Little girls will sing skip-rope rhymes about you." The abruptness of her laughter, its immodesty, set me back on my heels. I supposed that she had picked it up in the gutters of Hester Street and Mulberry Bend, where she went in search of wrecked lives to mend. The effort would beggar the skills of the ablest clock-smith in the land.

"I don't know what you must think of me." I thought she was referring to her guffaw, but that wasn't it. "Am I a hypocrite, Mr. Heigold?"

I took a sudden interest in a hangnail.

Eden's Clock   93

"Flowers in January, American Empire chairs, Morris Grafton wallpaper, Persian carpets. How ought one to live in the midst of so much human misery is a question I ask myself many times. I sold the silver and the Steinway, which I loved to play. Your eyes say I should do more." I shook my head vigorously. "What good did Saint Francis do the poor by becoming one? They need friends with money, Frederick, and not saintly exemplars of patient destitution."

I was glad to hear myself addressed as "Frederick." "Mr. Heigold" had sounded like a prelude to eviction.

LILIAN LIVED AS COMFORTABLY AS SHE COULD. SUSAN B. ANTHONY & MRS. STANTON—

"I knew both of them. I attended Elizabeth's funeral. Susan spoke just six words by way of eulogy, 'Well, it is an awful hush.' I suppose nothing else needed saying."

THEY DIDN'T STOP AT FLOPHOUSES WHEN THEY WENT ON LECTURE TOURS.

Holding the gardening shears thoughtfully, Mrs. Foster looked through the glass panes of the conservatory onto Park Avenue, where a variety of wheeled vehicles threw dirty slush onto the pavements.

"Have you read Henry James's things?"

SOME.

"Gramercy Park, Washington Square, Astor Place—James knows them intimately, every brownstone and fashion plate." She pointed the shears at

94 NORMAN LOCK

the passing parade of "types." "Like that cock of the walk strutting toward an assignation with his tailor or the elderly gentleman in the high silk hat, sparing a tender thought for his investments or last night's little supper at the Waldorf. Look at that grande dame walking her Pekinese. The pretty girl eating a napoleon is her niece. She'll be coming out in a year or two. She's still a child woman. If we were near enough, we could see the whipped cream on her chin. Fetching, isn't she, Fred? Or she will be when she ripens."

I kept my thoughts concerning ripe debutantes to myself.

"What awaits her? I wonder. A life of antimacassars and smelling salts. You need to look elsewhere for the real America."

We went inside and warmed ourselves at the gas fire in the sitting room.

"We must interest ourselves in how the other half lives." From an oak shelf, she took a book whose complete title was *How the Other Half Lives: Studies Among the Tenements of New York.* "His Honor Judge Carmody spoke more truthfully than he supposed when he declared the city to be a heartless place. He's a fool who has no business sitting on a bench, except in a park, where he can preside over the pigeons. Do you believe I exploit the poor?" Her tone of voice was a complication of emotions—partly hostile, partly sheepish, mostly, I'd have said, baffled. She was one of

Eden's Clock 95

those who will examine their every act for traces of a self-serving motive, as though it could be determined, as easily as milk that has soured, with a sniff. If that is martyrdom, then she suffered it.

In answer to her question, I shrugged ambiguously, without committing myself in pencil or chalk.

She went into the kitchen to make us tea. She didn't keep a cook or maid. A woman came to clean house, another to wash and iron; both had been inmates of City Prison.

Jacob Riis's book was known to me. How could it not have been to the husband of a reformer? Published in 1890, when he was a police reporter for the *New-York Tribune*, his exposés of tenement life and death stung anyone with a conscience. (Those without one would not be moved, except by the sight of lobster thermidor served on a gold platter.) By the light of his magnesium flash, Riis photographed cold or sweltering immigrant men, women, and children bent over piecework in gas-lighted sweatshops or packed into lice-ridden dens. Wide-eyed and fearful, they had the look of wild animals startled by safari hunters collecting specimens for a museum of horns and hides. Riis's book moved Theodore Roosevelt, of Rough Rider fame, to make poverty the cause célèbre of his term as New York City police commissioner. Ellen Finch had gone with Riis, Miss Stanton, and Miss Anthony to rescue a girl from a tenement basement on Baxter Street—too late; she soon died in Bellevue Hospital.

"When Jacob's book came out, a million people were jammed into thirty-seven thousand tenement houses in the Lower East Side," said Mrs. Foster, setting a tray on a walnut table. The cups were chipped, their gilt rims flaked. "I sold the bone china," she said, pride evident in her face and voice. Martyrs likely have an element of smugness in their makeup, which God wisely overlooks.

"Shall I be mother?" she asked, clutching the handle of the china pot.

I nodded that she should.

I sat on the Empire couch, its arms worn, its backrest stained with hair pomade, and let my mind drift with the steam rising from the cups, which might have been narcotic, so euphoric did I feel.

MAY I SMOKE?

"Please don't."

I felt a stab of resentment.

She would have noticed the petty storm of protest darkening the atmosphere. "If you wish, you can smoke on the balcony."

How good you are, Mrs. Foster! How lucky for me that you took notice of my plight, or I would be in solitary, searching for an ingenious method of escape or else, in Hamlet's words, of self-slaughter.

She followed me onto the balcony and surprised

me again, with the offer of a cigarette from a silver case. She held it open long enough for me to note the inscription, in Baskerville, inside the lid: *With Admiration, T. R.* "I don't allow cigars," she said, brushing snow from the iron railing with her bare hand. "Even from out here, the smoke will get into the drapes."

I put the stogy back in my pocket and smoked one of her black cigarettes. She talked about the down-and-out, whose desperation led them, oftentimes, to violence, drink, and a pauper's unceremonious burial on Hart Island or immersion in the East River. Like Lilian, she was no parlor reformer. The sun glared on the windows; on the apartments opposite, they flamed.

We went inside. I found it pleasant to sit and watch the shadows creep from underneath the heavy furniture. The evening breeze brought the smell of the river into the room through a partly opened French window. She paid no mind to the winter chill carried by the night air.

"You wish to go to San Francisco?"

I nodded yes.

"What would you do there?"

FIX A CLOCK.

"Aren't there enough clocks in New York to keep you busy?"

Ah, but E. Howard & Company makes a fine turret clock! I said to myself. I haven't had my hands inside one since Schenectady, seven or eight years ago, taking the Union College clock to pieces. Thomas Edison has a machine works there. Once, we sat at the same lunch counter. I was too shy to scribble I'M FREDERICK HEIGOLD, CLOCKSMITH. HOW DO YOU DO? (Topsy had not yet been fed cyanide-laced carrots, electrocuted, and, for good measure, strangled by a steam derrick.) Engrossed in a mechanical drawing, Edison paid scant attention to his ham sandwich and buttermilk, much less to me. A man like him knows that the rose sits waiting for someone with grit to pick it, careless of the thorns.

I dropped my cigarette into a crystal vase of purple asters.

Mrs. Foster watched as the cigarette paper unfurled in the pungent water. "I have a favor to ask."

I smiled to show my willingness to oblige.

"The Children's Aid Society is making up another orphan train to take homeless boys and girls out west for adoption. A number of them are living in the coal yards on East Fifth Street, between Lewis and the docks. If you help to gather them in, you can have a seat on the train."

Although I'd have preferred that she buy me a train ticket, I acquiesced.

"Lilian would be pleased," she said.

I guessed that she would be.

She opened an address book on her bird's-eye maple desk and wrote on a slip of paper:

> The Reverend Mr. Robert Winter
> Chapel of the Fallen, 2506 Pike Street
> (Near Sailors Exchange &
>   Hecker's Flour Mill)

"Mr. Winter is quite mad. He was desperately in love with Emily Dickinson, of Amherst. Have you heard the name? She's a poet few have read. She became a recluse, who talked to visitors from behind a screen. She died in '86, with few to mourn her. Robert never got over her. He rents a decrepit building, where he preaches to sailors, drunkards, frail sisters—those at the end of their rope. He blasphemes, damns heaven and the Beatitudes, without appearing to notice the incongruity. I suspect that his little flock treats it all like a variety show, with coffee and rolls served at the intermission."

I'LL GO SEE HIM.

"Tomorrow. At this time of night, he'll be getting ready to go out in search of bodies to save; I'm not sure that he believes in the soul. The homeless keep moving until dark, then flop wherever they can hide from the police, who will club them like scared rabbits or send them to the workhouse or the 'idiot' asylum on Blackwell's Island."

15

On the following morning, I stopped at the Chapel of the Fallen in time to hear the Reverend Winter preach to a congregation of six men and women, three asleep—an old woman with a cat shut up in a hand-basket, a Polish sailor, and a fellow beset by malaria or delirium tremens. The only person listening was a woman of thirty or forty, who would have been taken for fifty, worn and faded, dressed in a much-mended, though ironed, shirtwaist and pleated skirt. Her hair was a magpie's nest of ash gray curls threaded with two blue ribbons. She called to mind the Mother Goose rhyme:

> There was an old woman who lived in a
> shoe.
> She had so many children, she didn't
> know what to do.
> She gave them some broth without any
> bread;
> And whipped them all soundly and put
> them to bed.

Try as I might, I couldn't picture the Reverend Winter as a seminarian in love with a young poetess, who, from what Mrs. Foster knew of her life, had been bright, witty, and full of the devil. The old man looked like a figure in an allegory signifying lost hope. From what I could make of it, hopelessness was the text of his sermon, which he delivered sitting down. The chapel had been a grocer's store, and a faint smell of leeks persisted to remind his flock of life's savor, or else its squalor. What meaning we were meant to find in that chapel, I couldn't say. Maybe the woman in the shoe found comfort there. Maybe there was no meaning and no comfort to be had, except as one may take pleasure in rubbing salt into a wound that will not heal. I took a dislike to the Reverend Winter and could see no good in him.

"... and I say unto you, heaven is for Dives, if there is a heaven, and the rich man and his camel will pass through the eye of the needle. And there shall be rejoicing in heaven, if there is one. Riches will not rust nor costly garments be rent in sorrow, since the rich sorrow not, neither do they hunger nor thirst, and their costly garments are proof against the moth and time. Do not waste yourselves in hope, which is a sucker's game. Spend yourselves on the poor, instead, for so thou art and shall always be. Be not meek, for meekness will get you nothing. God loves the cheerful sinner and the sparrow. But you are not one of them. God is all-seeing and all-knowing; He is not, however, all-powerful. This is God's anguish, about which we can do nothing."

The sermon halted abruptly, as if Winter had

102   NORMAN LOCK

come to the end of his breath, or words, or passion. On second thought, passion didn't come into it. Even the sly minister of Dobbs Ferry's Presbyterian church, known for adjusting his outstretched hand to improve the effect of his pulpit oratory, could heat up a sermon and serve it piping hot, the better to fill the collection plates and tithing envelopes. Winter had no pulpit; he sat on a lyre-backed chair whose past life may have been spent in a Bowery saloon. His phrases were biblical, though bent to his own purpose; their inflection was flat, as if the words were exhausted of meaning, or else he was, in looking for one. At that time, he would have been Moses' age when he smashed the two tablets. The man sitting before me was a parody of the man of God.

After Winter's homily, I approached the woman, having a vague notion of pressing her hand or giving some other sign of recognition. But she began to put rolls in her string bag—for her children, perhaps. Not wanting to embarrass her, I gave my full attention to a mug of washy coffee. Even if we'd been able to speak to each other, I could no more have discovered the truth of her existence than a census taker. She looked at Winter, but his thoughts were elsewhere. She hurried out the door, turned the corner onto Cherry Street, and was soon lost from sight among the indifferent passersby.

I waited until the dreary little chapel was empty

Eden's Clock   103

of worshippers—I'll call them that to be kind—and went over to the reverend to introduce myself. MY NAME IS FREDERICK HEIGOLD OF DOBBS FERRY, BY WAY OF CITY PRISON. I PROMISED MRS. FOSTER TO HELP ROUND UP ORPHANS.

I looked into his old man's eyes, rheumy and myopic behind steel-framed eyeglasses, and saw perplexity. Whether caused by my sudden appearance in God's little grocery or by a hostile universe, none could have said. He seemed to swim up from the bottom of a lake whose depths sunlight could not sound. When he had shrugged off unconsciousness, I saw the resentment that I sometimes glimpsed in my own face, whose secrets are betrayed in the shaving mirror. Maybe I had interfered in his dream of Emily Dickinson, a flippant young woman of seventeen, studying Silliman's chemistry, geography, rhetoric, literature, and deportment at Mount Holyoke Female Seminary.

"*Why* have you come?" Winter asked peevishly.

Again, I showed him what I had written.

"Ah! Mrs. Foster is a fine woman! I don't give a damn if she's a Christian or not!" he said sharply, as if I had inquired into her spiritual condition. "She's good, as Christ militant would have it. The Sermon on the Mount was cold mush. The meek and the poor have had their fill of it!"

I recalled one of my mother's sayings: "When it rains porridge, hold up your dish."

"I wouldn't turn my other cheek, 'less it's to be kissed!" The old man's laugh was like the bark of a seal, hoarse and mirthless. His teeth were bad. "What did you say your name is?"

FREDERICK HEIGOLD.

"And you want to help gather the lost sheep?"

I nodded yes.

"By hook or by crook?"

Yes, again. I tried to wear a solemn face. The man was comical! But I've learned since that he had lived a rough life in the army and, for a long time after his retirement, on streets more crowded than Bombay's. He was an evangelist for a religion all his own, which may have been a necessary corrective to the good cheer of the Gospels, a reminder to God that our life is here and now. Like Emerson, whom he'd known, he believed that God and His heaven are centered in the gut. I remember his having said, "The seat of hunger and conscience is one and the same, and the two pangs are easily confused."

"I don't see how you can be of much use, Mr. Heigold, seeing that you can't speak. But I thank you, sir, for the offer." He disappeared behind a shabby curtain, which led to a room at the back of the chapel. I followed him inside.

"What more do you want of me?" Had he spoken angrily, or was it the peevish voice of the octogenarian?

A blackboard hung on the wall above a rolltop

Eden's Clock   105

desk. With the blue serge sleeve of Mr. Foster's old-fashioned suit, I rubbed out a line of Greek while Winter looked on—in amusement or bemusement, I could not have said. I pushed the rolling chair into the middle of the room and bid him sit facing the slate.

I WILL DO WHATEVER IS ASKED OF ME, MR. WINTER—OR DO YOU PREFER REVEREND?

"Mister is fine for all earthly undertakings; we'll leave the reverend to the devil. Let him break his teeth on my jerked flesh!" He barked again, his face brightening like a puddle in the sun coming out of the clouds. "Why is it so important for you to help an old sinner like me?"

MY WIFE WOULD HAVE WANTED IT. DID YOU KNOW LILIAN HEIGOLD? SHE WAS A NURSE IN GEORGETOWN DURING THE WAR. FOR A TIME SHE WAS WITH LOUISA MAY ALCOTT.

"I knew Miss Alcott. I was in the capital in late 1862, after the Union's harrowing defeat at Fredericksburg. We visited the Old Naval Observatory one rainy afternoon. She was very fine. Did Mrs. Foster mention that I was an army chaplain for most of my life?"

YES.

"Louisa had recently arrived from Concord, swept up on the tide of patriotic sentiment running at the full. There were many such at the time. I knew some of the Transcendentalists—not intimately, but well enough to stop at Waldo Emerson's house when I was in the village. I lived in Amherst before the war. I'm sorry, but I did not know your wife."

Heigold, you should hoof it to Grand Central, buy a ticket with the five bucks Mrs. Foster donated toward your reclamation, beginning with a proper bath and shave, and be on your merry way. This fellow is cracked.

Winter's eyes seemed brighter behind his round lenses, which, now and again, flared in the gaslight. The room was windowless. The Lower East Side had yet to be electrified. Candles, gas mantles, kerosene lanterns, and paraffin lamps were sufficient illumination for the other half. According to the lights of the well-to-do, the poor were created by God, and, by God, He should take responsibility for them!

"If you're determined to be useful, you can accompany Mr. Bonaparte tonight."

WHO IS MR. BONAPARTE?

"He's a black man who knows his way around the 'ghost world,' as he calls it—not that he has any truck with spiritual intercourse or mediums like Madame d'Esperance." He pointed to a pile of back issues of the *Spiritual Telegraph*. "He is invisible and knows where to look for vagrant children, whom society can't see through their opera glasses and pince-nez."

IS BONAPARTE HIS REAL NAME?

"It's a vexed question, sir, and one he has wrestled

Eden's Clock 107

with. He was only four or five years old when he was put on the block at Hill's Auction House in Richmond. He can't recall the name his mother gave him. The cracker who bought his papers shackled the child to his own last name and called him Bonaparte, after his favorite mule. He's a freedman now, although the Klan and Jim Crow would move heaven and earth to enslave him to fear, which just may be the strongest shackle of all. And so it is that my friend finds himself betwixt and between: On one hand, he despises the name he was given, along with a raggedy shirt and breeches; on the other, he takes pride in it. The phenomenon is not without precedent: Consider the transformation of a rugged cross on the Hill of Skulls into an object of worship."

I expect I gave him a quizzical look, because he went on to explain. "Our Mr. Bonaparte made the name his own, filled it with himself, so to speak."

I indicated that I understood.

"I'll introduce him as *Mr.* Bonaparte. He struck off his master's surname, along with his chains. Not knowing his father's name, he didn't take another. It's never straightforward, dealing with Negroes. They have long, tangled roots in the ground of this country. You'd better get some rest, Frederick; you've a wearisome night ahead of you." He jerked his thumb at a ladder in the corner of the room, leading to a hole in the ceiling. "Climb up 'Jacob's ladder' and find yourself a bed. My attic is cleaner than a seven-cent flophouse on Pell Street, and has no bugs, leastways none that draw blood."

16

After a nap, I climbed down from the attic and was greeted by Mr. Bonaparte himself. "How do you do?" He offered me his hand, which was large and, I fancied, could crack open walnuts. I hesitated to take it, as surgeons or musicians would, whose living, like mine, depended on the delicacy of their touch. Misunderstanding my reluctance, he spat on his palm and rubbed it on the white cloth of his shirt, as if to say, See, it doesn't rub off. Then he smiled and put me at ease. I offered him my hand, and he shook it without breaking my fingers.

"Mr. Frederick. Our friend the prime minister to the fallen has told me about you."

CALL ME FREDERICK OR FRED, I wrote on the blackboard.

"Mister, I will. But I can't extend you the same courtesy. Bonaparte may have been the name of an emperor, but it was also the name of Hardy's mule. He was the person who bought me. I wouldn't call him a man any more than he did me. He liked to joke to visitors that I was strong as a mule and dumb as an ox. Hardy liked a good joke. To watch a slave wearing an iron collar while trying to eat was great sport for him and his sons. A nigger in a nail barrel gave him fits. You know what that is? Don't bother writing, Frederick; it ain't worth chalk dust. You stick a black man in a barrel whose insides are a pincushion of tenpenny nails. They you roll it down a hill. Hardy called it a 'barrel of laughs.' Anyhow, Mr. Winter said that you want to help the children, only you can't talk. 'Good,' I told him. 'There's enough talkers in the world breaking wind.'"

We heard the street door open and close. We went into the front room as Winter was putting a net bag of groceries on the table that served as an altar when God was in the room. I remembered the "old woman who lived in a shoe." I hoped that she would be saved, although in my heart, I knew that she would not. The law of the land did not recommend mercy, unless those brought to the bar were named Jay Gould, James Fisk, or Thomas Durant.

"Will he do, Mr. Bonaparte?" asked Winter, unwinding a muffler from his scrawny neck.

"He will."

Winter set out bread and ham for our supper. "Mr. Bonaparte, some beer, if you please."

"My pleasure." He got a bucket from a cupboard and went out onto the street. Before the door had closed behind him, I heard children counting out:

110   NORMAN LOCK

Eeny, Meeny, Miny, Mo,
Catch a nigger by the toe,
If he won't work then let him go;
Skidum, skidee, skidoo.

"The German two doors down serves Ehret's lager," said Winter. "I'm partial to it." He set a sandwich on a plate in front of me, and an empty glass waiting to be filled. "You keep an eye out tonight, Frederick. The coppers are not all we have to worry about in our line."

Arriving with a pail of beer, Bonaparte filled our glasses. Swilling and chewing put an end to conversation. Having finished his meal, Bonaparte took a briar from his pocket, polished it on one side of his nose, packed it with Latakia tobacco, "a present from a Dutch merchantman from Utrecht for showing him Cornelius Vanderbilt's mansion," and smoked.

I lit a cigar that I'd found in Mr. Foster's coat pocket. The old man closed his eyes and savored my panatela, which, after so many years shut up in a closet, was as dry as a mummy's wrapper.

A commotion in the street broke into our reverie.

"There'll be a sliver of moon tonight. Perfect for our business," Winter said, rubbing his hands together. I thought of Fagin in *Oliver Twist* and shivered.

WILL THEY GO WITH US?

"The guttersnipes, maybe, though there be plenty

Eden's Clock   111

of sweet talkers with smooth faces and apples in their pockets who would keep them here. The older boys, the would-be hoodlums, are tough nuts to crack. They work for the gangs as alley rats, creepers, hoisters, porch climbers, and vestry thieves," said Winter, at ease in the colorful argot of crime. "The little ones may be persuaded by love, but the others don't know what it is and aren't incommoded by its absence."

Bonaparte produced a deck of cards. "Care to play a hand of flinch?"

I THINK I'LL STRETCH MY LEGS.

17

I walked south on Cherry Street and onto Fulton, heading toward the Brooklyn Bridge. I recalled the day that Lilian and I had bobbed like corks in a tide of gawkers come to see Barnum lead an elephant parade across the steel and granite behemoth to prove its strength to the cynics. Twenty years ago it was: May 17, 1884. The bridge stands, and all that has fallen from the great span are desperate creatures wanting to put an end to their misery in the East River.

I walked south on Pearl Street. Turning into Ferry Street, I sat on a low brick wall. Peck Slip and the East River were a stone's throw away. A woman walked toward me. She could have been any age. She wore a dress she may have fished from a barrel in

112   NORMAN LOCK

Ragpickers Row. It would have been new in the '80s, when a fashion plate from Park Avenue or Astor Place had worn it in Newport, where Commodore Vanderbilt kept his yacht and the nouveau riche waltzed. Dirty and bedraggled as it was now, the dress might have belonged to Mrs. Stuyvesant Fish, Mrs. William Backhouse Astor, or Mrs. John D. Rockefeller. In the Gilded Age, my mothballed suit of clothes and the Peck Slip scrubber's dress might have embraced on a dance floor in Niblo's Garden or in a boudoir on Fifth Avenue.

Outside a warehouse on Front Street, not far from the docks, some men stood around a steel tub, its inside tinned with copper. They were cooking meat— God knows what sort! Cat, dog, a haunch cut from a cart horse that had crumpled in the street. They invited me to join them.

I indicated that my gut was doing somersaults and my head about to split. I had no wish to sample a dish of doubtful provenance.

They flinched a step away from me. "Christ, you don't have something catching, do you, boyo?"

I shook my head and wrote TOO MUCH POP-SKULL.

"I ain't heard those dainty words since the war. Did you lose your squawk box to Johnny Reb?"

I nodded yes.

"Didn't they yell something fierce? It was enough to make the blood thin and the bowels shout 'Amen!'"

Eden's Clock   113

The others muttered in assent. They were all the right age to have shambled across fields of mud and slaughter.

I GOT MINE AT MANASSAS GAP.

They nodded knowingly, each carrying a gazette of battles and grim statistics in his head.

"I got fucked at the Bloody Angle," said the talkative one, whose name was Owens. He lifted his right trouser leg as delicately as a new husband would the hem of his bride's sateen shimmy. "They gave me a pretty fish-mouth stump. Before the war, I was a porter on the docks. Afterward, I was fit for nothing but rolling cigars. It got so my stomach griped at the smell of tobacco and the stink of Hebrews and Johnny Chinamen. I got nothing against them, mind. I'd have gagged on the Last Supper if it had been served up in a stinkhole!"

Owens poked at the wood in the tub, which had burned down into ardent coals, and spat in the grease that was dropping from the meat. It did smell good, and my stomach was beginning to rebel at the fastidiousness of my appetite. If horsemeat or possum was good enough for them, who was I to turn up my nose?

"My attorney wrote a letter on my behalf to Mr. F. P. Olcott, who sits, high and mighty, on the New York Stock Exchange. It was he who paid me three hundred dollars to soldier for his son. At the time, the deal was a good one in the eyes of a drudge who could not hope to see so many shin plasters all in a lump—no, sir, not if I lived to the ripe old age of the great begatters. Three hundred dollars, however, ain't— What's the word, Tolly?"

"*Compensatory.*"

"Compensatory for a blasted leg, even half a one, and would he please be so kind as to send me a— Tolly?"

"An emolument."

"Righto. Or if he preferred, a monthly allowance of, say, ten dollars. He did not—" He glanced at Tolly, who took a matchstick from his mouth and replied, "Deign."

"Deign to answer. I went to the dogs, I don't mind telling you, Mr. . . ."

HEIGOLD.

"Mr. Heigold. I suckled at the bottle, rye for preference. My sweetheart forsook me—"

"For cause," interjected Tolly.

"As did Mrs. Farley, my landlady, who turned me out of my rooms."

"Room," said Tolly.

"Don't be small, Mr. Tolliver!" To me, he explained, "Lawyers can't help but quibble."

"It takes legal knowledge and a keen mind to split a hair."

"I ended up on Blackwell's Island, which was just as well, for I was about to pawn my Jewett's leg. I

Eden's Clock   115

spent some time taking the air, so to say. Wonderful smell of pigs on the island from the swine farms in the Bronx. In God's own time, which is usually a right long pace, I was reformed by a Methodist lady who visited on Sundays and played the harmonium. I yelled like a reb to Jesus that I was saved! 'Glory Hallelujah!' Then and there I got down on my knees, which ain't easy if one of them has an iron hinge. The chief Bible-beater spoke glowingly to the warden of my reformation, and I was let go. Since that red-letter day, I've been here with my friends and associates, trying to keep body and soul together. Mr. Heigold, allow me to introduce Mr. Arlen Tolliver, Esquire, formerly of the law office of Abbett and Fuller, 229 Broadway."

"I was connected to the Jersey City office," said Tolliver with a self-effacing nod of his grizzled head. "How do you do, Mr. Heigold?"

I gestured that I did fair to middling.

"This gent used to play polo with the Rockefellers. Please be acquainted with Archibald R. Bostick."

"Mr. Heigold, a pleasure."

I returned the compliment with a smile.

"And last but not least, as the preacher said, this fellow is 'Lavender' Kennedy, who in a prior existence swept the halls of Tammany. How he came by such a colorful moniker is a story that must await another time."

116   NORMAN LOCK

Kennedy giggled like a fool.

"He hasn't been right in the head since he fell on it during the assault on Richmond. But Lavender is a good comrade, loyal and true, though he can't walk a straight line to save his life."

"He likes a sniff of ether now and again," observed Bostick.

Kennedy giggled once again.

"Wonderful stuff for neuralgia," remarked Tolliver.

"Meat's done," announced Owens, smacking his lips. "Archie, if you please." The two men lifted an iron grate from the tub on which the meat had been roasted. The tub tipped, and a live coal fell onto the dead grass, setting it aflame. Lavender Kennedy unbuttoned his fly and, in short order, had put the fire out.

"In his heyday, our Mr. Kennedy was a member in good standing of Hook and Ladder Company Number Eight," remarked Owens. "Gents, let's eat."

He and Bostick carried the grill into the warehouse and set it on a pair of trestles.

I followed them inside, where I was impressed by the furnishings.

"You're sure you won't have a slice of roast beef, Mr. Heigold?"

Roast beef! IF THERE'S ENOUGH TO GO AROUND, I WILL GLADLY.

"Make room, Tolly." With the flourish of a

Eden's Clock   117

cavalier taking off his hat, he gestured that I should sit.

CALL ME FRED.

"Have a seat, Fred—there, between the squire and Mr. Kennedy. Lavender, dear boy, shove over."

Owens served us each a slice of beef on a china plate. Although mismatched, the cutlery was genuine silver. Tolliver brought several jars of pickled items from a sideboard and, from an icebox, bottles of beer. "The beer is cold, Fred, ice being plentiful at this time of year."

"You seemed surprised by the elegance of our abode," said Bostick, whose manners were as polished as his patent-leather boots.

I gestured that indeed I was.

"The matter is easily explained," said Tolliver, who, I supposed, had been disbarred for playing fast and loose. "We steal from the feudal lords and robber barons of New York."

"I wouldn't have said 'steal,'" said Owens, having selected a pickled cauliflower. "But you're the pettifogger of our socialist commune. Have a cauliflower, Fred."

I speared one with my fork, which, I noticed, was engraved with the initials *H.V.* I wondered if it had once belonged to Henry Villard, the railroad magnate.

"It's no trick to purloin from the rich when one is invisible." Owens opened the door of a burled mahogany wardrobe. "They see only a menial. It may be a man from the butcher's, fish market, green grocer's, brewery, or greenhouse. It may be a man who's come to clean the furnace or a boy to sweep the chimney. It may be two men summoned to roll up a carpet and take it to be cleaned, or a ragged young fellow to unclog a stinking drain. Young girls, too, have their uses. We play a part. The rich see a costume, and nothing else. The carpet underneath your feet was carried off that way from the home of James Bailey, of Sugar Hill. Mr. Henry T. Sloan, of East Seventy-second Street, graciously provided the wall sconces; we arrived just before the men who were to install the new electric light fixtures could remove them. We grabbed the roast from the oven of Evander Berry Wall, a millionaire twice over by his twenty-first birthday. The papers ridicule him as 'king of the dudes.' He owns five hundred pairs of trousers and five thousand cravats. He will not miss a saddle of beef."

Having finished our supper, we opened the buttons of our waistbands. The fortunate among us admired the small noises indicative of good digestion. Lavender Kennedy belched, to which urbane Archie Bostick tut-tutted.

Owens put on a fancy smoking jacket and a velvet skullcap taken from a wardrobe and sat in a spindly upholstered chair, which looked old and foreign. On the table beside him stood a rack of the handsomest tobacco pipes I had ever laid eyes on. He gestured toward Tolliver, who, after a moment's deliberation, selected a honey-colored meerschaum, whose bowl had been carved with the self-satisfied face of a New Amsterdam Dutchman. Owens chose a clay pipe.

"A German clay, hand-rolled by Markus Fohr in the eighteenth century. I rarely smoke it—it's delicate—but I'm playing the gent for you. It came from the library of one of the codfish aristocracy, carried off inside a bolt of damask of doubtful provenance. Archie can play a draper to perfection. He sniffs, you know. Those fellas always seem like they've taken snuff."

My curiosity overcame discretion, and I asked, after my fashion, if they had a confederate in the houses that they robbed.

"Sometimes we do," replied Owens. "Sometimes we go in blind. We can always bluff our way out, if we must. But you'd be surprised how easy it is to purloin a small thing. Furniture must wait until the gentry are in Newport, the Adirondacks, or abroad making the Grand Tour—God rot them! Of course, we mustn't be greedy. Greedy is what *they* are. My friends and I are taking compensation."

"And rightly so," agreed Bostick.

The rich deserve to have their pockets picked, I told myself. The loss of a roast, a chair, or a soup tureen amounts to nothing in their books, although a housemaid or a kitchen boy might be blamed, lose his or her situation, or even end up in the Tombs.

"And what's your line of work, if the question is not an indelicate one?" asked Tolliver.

I MEND CLOCKS.

"As someone who has served time, I can't say I have much use for them," said Owens wryly.

"Is it a clock that has brought you to the East River?" asked Tolliver.

I'M VISITING A FRIEND. THE REVEREND WINTER. I chose not to elaborate on the complications of the two months since leaving Dobbs Ferry.

"We're familiar with him. He's something of a crackpot."

I kept my opinion to myself. Being mute has its advantages: It saves one from reckless remarks, idle comments, and dangerous commitments.

"I don't trust a man with such bushy eyebrows," said Owens.

I'M HELPING HIM FILL UP AN ORPHAN TRAIN.

"May God help you in your endeavor," said Tolliver, scraping the spent cake from the pipe bowl with a small pearl-handled pocketknife.

"We see many poor mites in our travels," said Owens, putting a paternal arm around Lavender Kennedy, who, for all he had to say for himself, could have been a mute, as well. "I don't often go by shank's

Eden's Clock 121

mare." He shook his leather leg at me. "I patronize the streetcars and elevated trains of our metropolis."

"There are two classes of poor mites," said Tolliver. "Street Arabs are older boys and girls who can fend for themselves. Guttersnipes are children of tender years, some as young as five or six, who are preyed on by bullies, drunkards, and religious maniacs who would strop a child into the Lord's Good Book."

Bostick took an apple from a drawer and offered it to me; I declined, and he set to eating it. His teeth looked sharp, and the apple delicious.

"Our Mr. Tolliver can always be relied on for a definitive answer. It's a pity you did that fiddling during the panic of '73. You'd be a chief justice now, if you'd walked the straight and narrow. But counselor is right: Of the two, guttersnipes need saving. They breed in the sewers and alleys. Summer brings them to the surface, like a hatch of mayflies, delectable to trout. We see less of them in winter. The street Arabs roundabout are another story. They are resourceful, cunning, and, when cornered, will fight tooth and claw."

"They enjoy the freedom of the streets," said Tolliver, folding his pocketknife.

"We give them little jobs to do," remarked Lavender Kennedy, breaking his silence. "Penny-candy stuff."

By the sharp look Owens sent his way, I guessed

that his contribution to the palaver was unwelcome. Owens cracked his knuckles. "Did you see our Mary Magdalene?"

I replied with a gesture of incomprehension.

"The fancy girl from Ferry Street. Her name is Mary Malloy, late of County Kildare. She was put out on her ear for—it's an old story that goes back at least as far as Potiphar's wife. In this case, it was Potiphar's son, who defamed Mary. You'd be shocked, Frederick, if I revealed the Potiphar by name! Do not ask; my lips are sealed."

Bostick put in an oar: "Ten thousand 'stem sirens' are said to walk New York City streets in search of—"

"What they will never find." Owens sighed.

"Prostitution is incorporated in thousands of commercial enterprises, all of them lawful."

"Right you are, Mr. Tolliver. And I should note that those modest entrepreneurs who do business on their backs do not have the same protections under law enjoyed by such enterprises. Throw me an apple, old son."

Bostick pitched one, and Owens bit into the crisp skin. I glimpsed a mouth enriched by several gold fillings.

"The flesh has been a problem ever since Eden." He ruminated a moment, then said, "But we do not judge our brothers and sisters, Fred. We leave that to those who are well paid for it."

I WAS LOCKED UP IN THE TOMBS FOR CONSPIRACY
TO COMMIT A PUBLIC OUTRAGE.

Although I immediately regretted the admission,
they seemed to look at me through new eyes. I imagined that they saw a man like themselves, determined
to "kick against the pricks," as is said in the Acts of
the Apostles.

"A moment of silence, gentlemen, as we remember the Haymarket massacre, May 4, 1886, in the
capital city of slaughter and butchery, Chicago. The
anarchists spoke in support of an eight-hour working
day; they spoke with sticks of dynamite. The sticks
were red. We mourn for all the dead."

"Amen," said Bostick, crossing himself in the
papist style.

Tolliver nodded in agreement, while Kennedy
began to scratch furiously in the vicinity of his
privates.

"It's the old blue ointment for you tonight, my
boy!" said Owens disapprovingly.

IT'S TIME I WAS GOING.

"Is it to be a night of hunting guttersnipes, Fred?"

Holding the apple as Eve would have when she
offered it to Adam, Owens fell silent a moment. "I
know where you can find a boodle of them."

He took a book from a shelf (an antiquarian's
edition of *Paradise Lost*, bound in crimson crushed
morocco), ripped out a blank page, and, on it,

sketched a map of South Street, from Peck to Pike Slips. "At South and Beekman Streets is the Fulton Fish Market. Behind the Flag Fish Company shed, a dozen urchins sleep in barrels. I imagine the mites are chilled to the bone this time of year."

I opened my watch to check the time and saw that the glass was cracked.

Turning his gaze from the apple in his hand to me, Owens smiled and said, "Like you, I am interested in timepieces." Opening a chest of drawers, he chose a watch from a dazzling row of them, an eighteen-karat-gold Patek Philippe. "For you."

Feeling my face flush with greed, I accepted the gift, knowing its immense value, even as I guessed its origins.

"Mr. Bostick, I think a drink is in order."

Bostick poured each one of us a large tipple of Glenfiddich.

"Ah!" said Tolliver, smacking his lips. "I do love the delicate taste of pear!"

"Divine!" said Owens, producing a weird music by running his finger, wet with whiskey, around the rim of his glass. He wore on one of them a fat gold ring.

THIS IS VERY GENEROUS OF YOU. MY THANKS.

Owens nodded and moved his hand like a Pope distributing alms.

I stuffed the gold watch in my pocket and saluted

them each in turn. All but Kennedy solemnly returned it. He guffawed wondrously, so that I had a view of his molars. As I was leaving, he surprised me by wishing me "Happy hunting!"

"Be of good cheer, ye doers of good works! Guttersnipes will be with us always," said Owens by way of farewell.

"Amen to that," said Tolliver, nosing his glass of Glenfiddich.

Night had blackened the East River. On the Brooklyn hills across it, lights, antique and modern, had been put on to welcome the sailor home from the sea, the carpenter, the shoemaker, and the judge from their benches, and the children from work or play, all save the forty thousand homeless ones. I headed back to Winter's chapel. At Cherry Street and Mechanics Alley, a man was smoking out a wasp's nest underneath the eave of his house with a burning newspaper.

18

On Pike Street, gutters overflowed with shadows as the gaslights bloomed above the pavements. The crèche in the chapel window was a shambles of plaster of Paris sheep. The shepherds lay in a heap, while the three wise men, stroking horsehair beards, seemed puzzled by the infant Jesus lying in a manger without a head on His shoulders. Only the blue-gowned and wimpled Mother of God appeared serene. Perhaps I'd drunk too much Glenfiddich, but I heard her say, "None of this matters; what you see here is a clumsy attempt to show the ideal. The time you hold so dear means nothing, either. Your Patek Philippe—*with twelve complications!*—and E. Howard & Company's turret clock get no closer to the truth of the absolute than this silly display!"

I went inside the chapel, to find an Indian dressed in a flannel suit sitting on one of the wire-backed chairs. An old trilby hat rested on his lap.

"Mr. Frederick Heigold, please be acquainted with John Jemison of the Seneca people," said Bonaparte. "His great-grandfather's name was Fen-nis'-hee-yo, but white men are fond of baptizing aliens in the same way that they give Christian names to mountains, rivers, and entire continents. I wonder how the lunarians feel when they go boating on Smyth's Sea. His family, by the way"—he gestured toward the Indian—"is buried under Olmsted's Central Park."

I shook Mr. Jemison's hand, a gesture understood by all conditions of humankind.

"John is, like you, a graduate of the Tombs, after having set fire to cigar-store Indians up and down Broadway."

"It makes me sore as hell every time I see one," he said, screwing up his face.

"Our Seneca friend does a little scouting for us."

Eden's Clock 127

"Five boys are living in an empty vault, inside a burned-out bank on Wall Street," said Jemison, giving his water-stained hat an urgent thump.

I put Owens's sketch of a map in Bonaparte's hand. With paper and pencil, I told him that homeless boys could also be found at the Fulton Fish Market, which is not so far from the chapel as the bank at New and Wall Streets. Besides, a vault offered better shelter from the cold than a barrel and did not smell of cod.

"The fish market it is, then," said Bonaparte. "Thank you, friend John. We'll see each other again soon."

The man put on his hat and left the chapel.

WHERE IS MR. WINTER?

"The old man's asleep. He's been feeling poorly."

Bonaparte and I walked to South Street, then turned toward the bridge and the market just beyond it. The remnant evening light was draining from the western sky. A wind picked up and brought the smell of the river. Shivering with cold, I turned up my coat collar. Not a night to be sleeping in a barrel, I thought.

"They flop not where they like, but where they can," said Bonaparte. "The papers picture them happy as larks, until they scream for their removal from the streets they befoul with their unwashed presence. I've seen tykes asleep in hallways and the cellars of fleabag hotels, inside old boilers, in derelict boats beached or

128   NORMAN LOCK

abandoned at a run-down wharf. They like subway entrances and steam gratings in the cold months. I've seen them wriggle into places God long ago forgot. The coppers roust them with their sticks, and the child snatchers make white slaves of them. New York is a city where a flower girl peddling nosegays in front of the opera house might be a child prostitute and a ten-year-old boy shoveling shit in a pigsty could be an apprentice pickpocket or a cutthroat. Once, I heard a rich man standing on the granite steps of the stock exchange growl, "There ought to be a pint-size electric chair for snot-nosed brats!" Bonaparte spat, a gesture rich in significance, as well as germs.

We picked our way through a pitch-dark alley behind the Flag Fish Company and then, on tiptoe, sidled up to a row of open barrels. The night seemed to hold its breath; not a cat in heat or a watchman walking his beat disturbed the silence. Bonaparte unshuttered the lantern, ready for guttersnipes to spill out of their rank hideaways, shining, miraculously, in fish scales. Would shoes, hot food on a plate, and a clean bed within four walls be enticement enough to overcome their mistrust of men?

A whistle blew, loud and shrill. Voices barked, a door was thrown open, and the police were upon us. The barrels, I saw, as Bonaparte and I turned and ran for dear life, were empty. Bonaparte hurled the lantern at our pursuers. The flaming kerosene spread

Eden's Clock   129

across the mouth of the alley. The policemen jumped back, giving us time to beat it down the cobblestone landing and hide beneath the pier. Even now, my hand recalls the ring of seaweed and mussel shells attached to a slippery piling beside me. Small waves tripped over our boots and soaked our trouser bottoms. The water was cold.

Bonaparte and I remained stock-still. For how long, I couldn't have said. There was no light for me to read the dial of my Patek Philippe, which I fretted over foolishly, careful that it shouldn't get wet or, because of a stumble, broken. After He had set time going, like a midwife slapping a newborn baby's bottom, God would have worn such a divine timepiece as He went about the business of creation. Finally, Bonaparte and I left our hiding place and crept along the shore. We passed a line of fishing boats waiting for the outgoing tide.

Once again, our hearts were made to jump by the strident pitch of a whistle. Three lanterns were swinging in the dark not thirty yards from where we stood in the shadow of a coastal schooner. Yellow light was licking at the cobblestones and would shortly engulf us. Bonaparte grabbed my wrist and pulled me into a leafless forest of masts swaying against the night sky, where ships rode the river's oily swells.

"Come out, you bastards! Let's see what sort of pricks like to diddle little kids."

130   NORMAN LOCK

I caught a glimpse of Bonaparte's eyes, which shone briefly in a beam of light thrown by a lamp swinging from a yardarm. They were wide with terror. Mine would have been the same. The cops might have laid us out then and there with their billy clubs. Bonaparte shrank from the lamplight, and I with him.

"Check every crate and barrel. Jenkins, you and Heine get your asses down under the pier. And the dummy with the fancy watch is mine."

The lights dispersed in the dark and sailed off like fireflies into the corners of the night. Unseen by us, the water slapped against the rocks.

Heavy with the weight of the present, which contains the whole of time past, the Patek Philippe was—minute by minute—chaining me to a dreadful future. Afraid to be caught with stolen goods, I reached into my pocket, intending to toss the watch into the river, but I couldn't bring myself to do it. Was it for this that Owens had been generous? I asked myself.

We found a boat made fast to an iron stake. We cast off, lay down in the bottom, and let the river have its way with her, until we were well away from the beaters on the pier. This is Owens and Tolliver's doing, I told myself as I began to row. Was it to spite me or Mr. Winter? Not until later did it occur to me that they were protecting their commercial territory from do-gooders who disturbed the rat's nests from which they profited, as Fagin and Bill Sikes had done in Dicken's London Town, in the shadow of Newgate Prison.

Softly, the snow began to fall, lightly covering Bonaparte and me, where we lay cradled at the bottom of the small boat, rocked gently by the East River, which is neither fresh nor salt, attesting to the truth of a world that is neither all one thing nor another.

19

Putting our backs to it like a pair of galley slaves shackled to each other, we reached Governor's Island, in New York Harbor. Red Hook lies to the east, across Buttermilk Channel. Farther south, the East River pours into Lower New York Bay through the Narrows, separating Brooklyn and Staten Island. Ten miles due south, at Sandy Hook, the river's atoms mingle with those of the Atlantic Ocean as brine gives way to salt. Shivering in our damp clothes, we waited for sunrise.

Bonaparte stretched his legs and sighed. "We're in a pickle, Frederick. I wish I knew who dropped us in the barrel." Early-morning light glinting on the crystal of my watch caught his eye. "Now there's a pretty item! I don't recall seeing it before. How did you happen to come by it?" His voice betrayed his suspicion.

I wasn't to blame, Jack, for the pickle barrel. But what good would come from telling the tale of a mute

132   NORMAN LOCK

man fallen among thieves? I opened my hands and shrugged off responsibility for our predicament.

"Being dumb has its advantages, I suppose," he said before turning on the Almighty for having made us slaves to thirst. "It would've been better if He'd created us in the image of the camel." If God was in the mood to be merciful, He would forgive the blasphemy of a man who was tired, cold, and, to pile on the agony, the object of a manhunt. "I had the dogs on me once before," said Bonaparte. "I don't intend getting treed a second time."

I waited to hear the tale of his escape from bondage, but he didn't seem inclined to tell it.

"The old man said you were on your way to Frisco when they threw you in the Tombs."

I nodded yes.

"I've never been west of the James River. I'm thinking I could use a change of scenery. Any reason why I shouldn't keep you company?"

I had known him for a day and a night—that is to say, I knew him not at all. But if not for him, I'd have been in a City Prison cell or on the river bottom with a broken skull. He was shrewd, resourceful, and strong, as men are who live rough until sickness, whiskey, or a knife puts an end to them. You know the sort, Jack. I'd say that you are one of them.

"Unless you're going back to Dobbs Ferry . . ."

My mind's clockwork balked at any movement

Eden's Clock   133

save forward. I gave my hand to Bonaparte, who took it in his black one.

The morning breeze whipped the harbor into chop. Ecstatic seabirds dropped like stones to spoon up spots and rainfish in their bills. We walked beneath chestnut and hickory trees, from which the island took its original name of Nutten Island, till we came to Fort Columbus. At that moment, America had no enemies, unless the Order of the Star Spangled Banner feared attack by suffragists. I pictured Susan B. Anthony waving her red shawl and feisty Amy Bloomer dressed in khaki pants, aboard a dreadnought steaming into New York Harbor, while the ghost of Elizabeth Cady Stanton fired broadsides and pamphlets from her plot in Woodlawn Cemetery at the blockheads in the Capitol.

We stopped beside a wall brightened by scarlet pokeberry leaning against a plastering of snow. Wanting worms, a lone robin, another fugitive from its tribe, monotonously complained. A soldier, his teeth stained by chaw, was parsing the verb *fuck* for the benefit of a man of lesser rank. Fed through the mangle of his brogue, it came out *fook*. It was all "fook this" . . . "fook that" . . . and "fook the other t'ing!"—a discourse punctuated by squirts of tobacco juice on the pockmarked snow.

"For fook's sake, man, I'm dyin' for a drop!" cried Bonaparte, whose glib tongue slipped into the patter of the Irish, whom ignoramuses call "green niggers." "I'm *that* cold, I am!"

The older man handed him a flask from his coat.

"I'm obliged, Sergeant, for my bones' sake." He took a swig and returned the flask, but not before wiping its mouth on his sleeve. "Now, I'd not say no to a little plain water after the strong. I'm perishing of thirst!"

I gestured, theatrically, that I, too, was parched.

"Mr. Heigold can't speak, having given his voice to the cause, but he'd be glad of a cup of water to wet his lips."

The sergeant, whose name was Kelly, led us through an iron door, down a flight of stairs, and into a kitchen, where some soldiers were preparing a meal while others were scrubbing pots and a lieutenant, his head on his arm, was sleeping at a table slippery with peels. Bonaparte and I were each given a tin cup of water and a plate of boiled potatoes and peas.

"You saved our lives, Sergeant Kelly. Bless you for it! Now if you have any to spare, the pair of us would be grateful for the loan of some dry clothes."

Kelly took us to the quartermaster, who was smoking a church warden. He didn't look like a soldier, leastways not one of ours. He wore old-fashioned side-whiskers and an Ottoman field marshal's red tarboosh on his head, which gave him an air of a pasha.

Eden's Clock   135

"Aloysius, fix up these two shipwrecks, if it pleases your good self."

Taking our measure with an expert eye, he pulled two pairs of dungarees and two wool coats from a shelf. "Put these on." Next, squinting through tobacco smoke, he sized up our feet. "These'll do," he said, setting before us army regulation boots and socks.

"And a roof for your thatch," said the genial Kelly, presenting us with slouch hats.

"We're grateful to you. My friend and I very nearly took the bath to end all baths," said Bonaparte, signing on to the idea of shipwreck, more plausible than the truth behind our arrival on Governor's Island, where the fort stood guard over the bay.

Dressed like a pair of ragtag misfits, we followed Sergeant Kelly outside to smoke and palaver like three men, well met, on a pleasant day. We might have been menials taking a break from polishing brass stair rods at the Breakers, while our gold-buttoned, blue-flanneled betters were sailing aboard their yachts on Narragansett Bay.

"Where were you two heading before the mishap?" asked Kelly.

With a stick, I wrote SAN FRANCISCO in the snow.

"By any chance is there a ship that could take us there?" asked Bonaparte.

"Not that I know of. There *is* a three-master making for Cuba this afternoon. She's sitting at Red

136   Norman Lock

Hook, on the other side of Buttermilk Channel. I'll get a brig rat to row you across, if you care to change your heading."

"We're beholden to you, Mr. Kelly."

"No trouble at all, gents! You could say Red Hook's my personal commissary. The rat will row me back a bottle or three of Van Brunt's antifogmatic. It's good for what ails you."

We waited on the pier to be taken across the channel to Brooklyn. Bonaparte kicked at a dock cleat with his new boots, scratched a stubbly cheek, and gave every appearance of a man uneasy in his mind.

"I'm a con man, Fred," he said at last. "I sing and dance and fool the world."

He would have seen disapproval in my eyes, because he went on, with some bitterness. "Maybe you think a black man should show more dignity. Such noble qualities are hard to hold on to after you've worn a collar or had your neck scratched by a twist of Kentucky hemp. Why must the Negro always be a special case?" Looking across the water, his eyes glazed over, as if they beheld the promised land. "We have our own way of dealing cards in a white man's game."

He glared at me to show that he would not be shamed or cowed. "I have a beautiful hand; you couldn't tell it from a notary's or a copy clerk's. I became quite an accomplished forger and would be

Eden's Clock   137

still if I hadn't tried to sell the Brooklyn Bridge, so to speak. I was caught, tried, found guilty of a felony, and spent eight years up the river in Sing Sing, where I read a number of fine books given to me by your wife. It's for her sake that I saved your ass."

WHY DIDN'T YOU SAY?

He could see that I was angry. "You learn not to lay all your cards on the table. First, I wanted to see what sort of white man you are." He shrugged. "An old habit."

I stood there, dithering and wondering whether I should forget all about Mr. Wallace and his clock.

"It's wise to keep moving, Fred. You'll either reach your destination or arrive at a better one. In San Francisco, I'd be just another bootblack."

I spat into the river. The gob neither advanced nor retreated. Is time in abeyance? I asked myself. If I were to open my watch, would I see that the hands have stopped? If I put it to my ear, would I hear the silence that rounds our little lives?

"What do you say, Fred? Will you go with me to Cuba? They've got clocks there, too."

20

The *Eloise* sat low in the water of Gowanus Bay. Lacking sheet-metal stacks, she looked old-fashioned among steamers and packet boats dirtying the winter sky above the river with their coal smoke. She appeared seaworthy, as far as I could tell, who was a sailor insofar as having ridden the ferry and twice read *Moby-Dick* could make me one. Bonaparte and I walked out on the dock and called to a man on the schooner's quarterdeck, who was barking orders through a megaphone. By his cap and demeanor, he would have been the captain.

"Hallo! What do you two want here?"

"We're looking for passage south!" shouted Bonaparte through his cupped hands.

"We don't take on passengers."

Steam cranes were hoisting blocks of sandstone from the *Eloise*'s hold; these would be carved into Tuscan columns and balustrades for a grand boathouse in the classical style going up beside the Lullwater, in nearby Prospect Park.

"We can make it worth your while," said Bonaparte shrewdly.

My head fairly swiveled on my neck as I glanced at him; we didn't have two cents to rub together.

"What, in your estimation, is worth my while?" asked the captain, his eyes narrowing, either in greed or in a squint caused by the sun glaring on the water, which made the sandstone sparkle.

Bonaparte took the Patek Philippe from his coat. "This item is worth a small fortune."

I had only a hopping-mad charade to express my

Eden's Clock　139

ire at having my pocket picked, and Bonaparte paid it no notice. His eyes were fixed on the captain leaning over the railing above us. He came down to join us on the pier.

"It's a watch such as a crowned head would carry. A well-known mogul was the last to possess it before it came into the hands of my friend here. Don't ask him how; he spoke his last words at Manassas Gap and cannot say. This article is worth more than you'd earn going 'round the Horn."

I should have snatched the watch from the procurer's hand, turned my back on both of them, pawned it, found the Magdalene, and treated her to a steak dinner. But I was caught in the works, and the deadbeat escapement permitted no backsliding.

"Agreed," said the captain, accepting the watch.

"Meals and rum included?"

"I'll treat you like a couple of Rockefellers as far as Florida."

Bonaparte rubbed his hands together like a fly eying a spoonful of jam.

"My name is Bock, captain of the *Eloise*."

"Mine is Bonaparte; this gentleman who can't speak is Frederick Heigold."

"An emperor and a dummy." He glanced at me. "No offense intended."

Bock showed us to the ship's only first-class cabin, kept for important traders in sugar and tobacco.

140   NORMAN LOCK

Bonaparte and I would surrender it at St. Augustine to Mr. Orville Smith, of the Havana-American Company, for his six-hundred-mile trip to the Cuban capital of America's unofficial province in the Caribbean. Granite blocks left in the hold, white and gritty as sugar cubes, would be raised by William Otis's steam shovel and African-Cuban sweat into a monument to the spirit of revolution—an American hotel or a national bank.

Night had already unpacked its cargo of darkness when the *Eloise* got under way. She sailed easterly, rounded Sandy Hook point, then struck south. Off Gunnison Beach, she caught a favorable wind that carried her into the Atlantic. She would keep six miles offshore, stopping at Norfolk and Savannah to take on fresh water, until she arrived at the St. Augustine inlet of the Matanzas River, nine hundred miles from New York Harbor.

"How long do you expect the trip to take?" asked Bonaparte.

We were sitting in the wardroom, eating potato pancakes. Bock was devoted to them and would rouse the poor cook at any hour to unlimber his skillet.

"Ten days, maybe less, maybe more. No more than twelve. The *Eloise* is a sailing vessel, gentlemen, not a steamer. We're at the mercy of the wind and currents. She's a good lady, and she'll see us safely there. What do you think of cook's potato pancakes?

Eden's Clock   141

He's from Saxony, and no place on earth does them better. I could eat them morning, noon, and night, and sometimes I do. Being a captain has advantages. I swear I'd sooner get rid of my first mate than my Saxony cook."

Following her husband's death in the May 1849 Dresden uprising, Bock's mother had emigrated, along with her two young sons, from Saxony to a small fishing village on the New England coast. The elder brother became a sailor in the U.S. Navy and, later, was blown to smithereens aboard the battleship *Maine.* "Such a crime was committed never before in hist'ry; / A loud report, down went the ship, all was enshrouded in myst'ry." That ripe tripe had gusted through the swinging doors of taprooms across our blessed land during the winter of 1898.

"I've led a peaceful life, though one not without incident," said Bock, carrying his empty plate to the hatch opening onto the galley. "At sixteen, I went to sea and have had my share of scrapes, shipwrecks, and Caribbean pirates, who were too soused with rum to do us harm."

Jack, you would have met such men as Captain Bock when you sailed to the Orient for William Randolph Heart's newspapers to cover the Russo-Japanese War.

"The *Eloise* isn't my first ship; before her, I was captain of a steam launch running arms from

142   NORMAN LOCK

Jacksonville to the revolutionaries through the American blockade of Cuba. McKinley did his best to keep us out of war, but the sinking of the *Maine* made the public see red. We had been putting correspondents ashore for the *New York World* and the *New York Evening Journal*. The launch sank in Santiago Bay after a Spanish gunboat rammed her. We spent the night clinging to packing crates, until the *Peoria* fished us out of the water."

An American expeditionary force drove the Spaniards out of Cuba in the interest of the United Fruit Company and the American Sugar Refining Company. Bananas and Domino sugar would be the making of white-skinned Cubans of Spanish descent. Those who were the product of Spanish colonizers and African slaves, as well as a hundred thousand Chinese immigrants from America imported to do the coolie work, would not taste the sweetness of life, only its bitterness. The sanctimonious windbags in Washington considered the Cuban revolutionaries incapable of governing themselves. Isn't that always the way, Jack?

We had followed Bock down into the *Eloise*'s hold. "They say the whitest granite in the world is cut from the Bodwell quarry in Hallowell, Maine. This is the same stone they used to build the Tombs," he said to me, as if my recent incarceration were written on my face. "Feel the smoothness of its skin."

That granite block was more pleasant to the touch than the skin of a peach.

"How came you two mugs to be in Red Hook?"

"Seeing the sights," replied Bonaparte as readily as a schoolboy tells a stretcher.

The captain bit his lower lip, as though he intended to say something not altogether in our favor, then decided against it. We would have seemed suspicious characters in his eyes—what with our fancy watch and fanciful tale.

"Tomorrow, we put in to the Norfolk docks." He looked at his new watch with the avidity of a jeweler contemplating the Koh-i-Noor diamond. "While the crew unloads a sandstone block, I believe I'll have this article appraised."

By the strength of his gaze, I guessed that he suspected Bonaparte and me of being a pair of pennyweighters or dips. A graduate of the New York City "knowledge box," I'm literate in the language of an underworld where neither ancient Greek nor Latin is spoken.

"Either of you boys care to see the sights of Norfolk?"

"I give a wide berth to towns that flew the Stars and Bars."

"What about you, Heigold?"

I said yes with a nod of my head.

21

That night, the *Eloise* rounded Fisherman Island, a quarantine station off the tip of the Delmarva Peninsula. The wind being fair, she spanked across twenty miles of water and into the mouth of the James. Running between Willoughby Spit and Fort Monroe, she entered the Elizabeth River. After a five-mile sail, we made Norfolk Harbor at Craney Island, not far from where the Union navy had scuttled the steam frigate *Merrimack* during the evacuation of Norfolk. Confederate engineers later salvaged her engines and hull. Converted into an ironclad, she fought the Union ironclad *Monitor* to a draw in the Battle of Hampton Roads. Captain Bock was well versed in naval history.

In the morning, he and I walked into Norfolk. On Yarmouth Street, three blocks from the harbor, a Brobdingnagian pocket watch emblazoned with *Anthony Hodder, Horologue*, caught our eye, its gold-painted tin creaking in a landward breeze.

"How can I help you, gentlemen?" inquired the proprietor, bent over a mantel clock. I had the odd sensation that I was looking at myself presiding over a universe taken to pieces—the familiar wheels, gears, screws, and pins neatly arranged on the bench, while

Eden's Clock 145

a Lilliputian's tools waited for my expert hands to put things right.

Bock slid the pocket watch across the counter.

Hodder picked it up, his excitement barely contained. "A Patek Philippe!" He pulled the loupe over his eye and took a good squint. "I've never seen one before. It's a gorgeous thing! It has twelve complications, you know." He sat on his stool behind the counter and indulged the refined sensibility of the artisan who works with rare materials. Time is the rarest of all, and the most obdurate.

Bock looked pleased. "It's the real McCoy?"

"No question. Listen." He held the watch to the captain's ear. "The music of the spheres clatters in comparison."

"What's it worth?"

Hodder glanced at Bock as a priest at the Communion rail would have at a man who takes chaw tobacco from his mouth before eating the body of Christ.

"If you're thinking of selling it," he replied tartly, "I can't afford it."

"Lately, it's been roughly used," said Bock, looking askance at me as Hodder pulled a face, partly incredulous, partly horrified. "Do you think it should be oiled?"

"It's not a threshing machine!" He paused to compose himself. "I wouldn't attempt such a thing. God

146   NORMAN LOCK

forbid I made a mistake. I'd never forgive myself." He held the watch in his hand as if it were a disk pried from a dead martyr's spine.

Bock took the watch from Hodder, who parted with it reluctantly. "I'd never forgive you, either." He opened his wallet and took out a two-dollar bill. "I thank you for your trouble, sir."

Outside in the street, the captain clapped me on the back. "To think I thought you and your friend were shysters!"

I smiled, wondering if maybe we weren't.

We stopped at Arnold's Lunchroom, on Boush Street, across the railroad tracks from the Imperial Guano Company's brick building on the river's eastern branch. It was a long, narrow place, set between an insurance brokerage and an undertaker's parlor. "Life and death, there's fuck all in between!" Tolliver had said as much in Manhattan four days prior to my taking in the sights of Norfolk.

Only four days ago, I had sat in Fagin's den on Fulton Street and eaten roast beef stolen from a Park Avenue kitchen. Three months had passed since I'd studied the effects of drowning on the face of a young black man in Dobbs Ferry. All my days, I had been nailed to the rack of time, screwed to its chassis, bolted to its axle, bound hand and foot to its turning wheel. Time had been my element, as necessary as water. It had passed through my hands like a silken cord,

Eden's Clock   147

which could as easily set off a handsome woman's neck as strangle it. But at a table in Arnold's Lunchroom, across the street from a purveyor of bird shit, I had slipped from its grasp. I felt lost, Jack, the way a man would feel on a raft, at the mercy of currents outside his ken.

"We'll have beefsteak and oysters, with Michelob to wash them down!" shouted Bock to a pasty-faced waiter wearing a Simon Legree mustache as we sat at a table underneath a framed photograph of a Confederate soldier astride a horse. I could tell that the captain was itching to ask me about my past, but his natural curiosity was belayed by New England reticence. He told me that he was a Mainer, raised at Prout's Neck, on the Atlantic Ocean, twelve miles south of Portland.

"There's a painter there named Winslow Homer. Ever hear of him? Slightly built fellow. He'd been a real dude in his younger days. I could see a trace of it in his expression, though the snootiness had been smoothed away, not smoothed so much as rubbed— better yet, ground on a carborundum stone."

Anyone who had turned the pages of *Harper's Weekly* would have been familiar with Homer's engravings of postbellum beauties in crinolines, their fresh faces shaded by parasols from the summer sun as it fell on New Jersey seaside towns. His illustrations left me flat. His Civil War paintings, however, which

148 NORMAN LOCK

I'd seen at the National Academy of Design, were strong, though tepid in comparison to photographs taken by Mathew Brady and Alexander Gardner of Civil War bloodbaths.

"Last fall, I put the *Eloise* into dry dock at the Pine Point shipyard to have her bottom painted. I took the ferry across Saco Bay to Prout's Neck to visit my family. Early one morning as I was letting the dog run on the beach, I came across him sitting on a camp chair, near enough to the breakers for them to put a slick on his oilskin and sou'wester. Old man though he was, he kept his back straight as a mast. A sketchbook on his lap, he was careless of the salt spray. The air was wet with it, and damned cold, too."

He fell silent as his eyes beheld something far away and, if I read his face aright, sad.

Whatever he was thinking, he kept it to himself. He shook off his reverie, and, lifting the last oyster shell to his lips, he let the animal slip down his gullet. They were good oysters, tender, fat, and sweet. The steaks had been first rate, too. We couldn't have eaten better at Delmonico's, although Arnold's napkins were cheap cotton, and the tablecloths sheets of newsprint.

While Bock mopped meat juice from his plate with a heel of bread, I read, on the front page of the

Richmond Times–Dispatch, a few items that had not been drowned in grease and brine.

TEDDY ON COLOR-LINE

"INSULT TO THE WHITE BLOOD."

**Mr. Roosevelt Intimates That He Will
Continue to Appoint Colored Men to
Office, North and South,
Without Regard to Objections to Them
Solely on Account of Their Color.**

And there was this curiosity reported from Nice, on the south coast of France:

CRAZY MILLIONAIRE!

Mr. Yturbe, the eccentric millionaire who fears the light of day and shuns a draught like a plague because of a "witch's" prophecy, continues to be an object of great interest at Monte Carlo. His latest fad has been to equip his palatial villa at Cimiez with an enormous lift, into which his closed, curtained, and shuttered carriage is driven, and in this way he reaches his darkened, heavily draped apartments, which are kept at Turkish bath temperature.

"INTERCOLLEGIATE SOCIALISTS"

All over the country there is a warm discussion of the new methods of propaganda employed by the socialists—by one of our "57 varieties" of socialists. This method is the issuance of a circular letter to college students proposing the organization of an Intercollegiate Socialist society. The letter is signed by ten well-known names, among them that of Jack London. It would look as though the colleges, strongly "inclined to the existing order of things," were going to be chary of encouraging the spread of the views held by this new committee of ten; but Jack London has been given the opportunity to present his views to the students of the University of California, and these are the words used by this "strong" writer: "You are drones that cluster around the capitalistic honey vats. Your fatuous self-sufficiency blinds you to the revolution that is surely, surely coming, and will as surely wipe you and your silk-lined, puffed-up leisure off the face of the map."

You take no interest in honey vats, Jack. But is there no other way for you to feel alive, except by

Eden's Clock   151

rubbing yourself raw and then, for good measure, salting the tender places? No man willingly lays himself open to pain so far beyond the ordinary. Is it for the glory of literature that you hunted seals in the Bering Sea, gold in the white silence of the Yukon, and news for the *San Francisco Examiner* of the Japanese army's subjugation of Korea and its defeat of Russia by the Yalu River? Or may it be that the reason for living is hidden even from yourself, as if civilization were still in its infancy?

I looked up from the newspaper in time to see Bock, who'd been nursing a small Bacardi rum, poke his tongue into the glass to retrieve the last amber drop at the bottom.

"Time we were getting back to the *Eloise*," he said.

We were heading toward the pier when he suddenly pulled me into a haberdashery shop. "You look like you crawled out of a scupper. Let's get you set up with a new rig. Don't fuss, Fred! I can afford to be generous, by God I can!" He patted the buttoned pocket where the watch was stowed.

"Smarten up my friend!" he shouted to a youngish fellow wearing a tape around his neck and a nankeen vest bearing chalk marks like my own.

The shop assistant would have been used to bellowing sailors and captains. He yawned like a hippopotamus ready to accept peanuts from visitors to the zoological garden. He took his time, nibbling a fingernail as he sauntered toward us. With the jadedness of a coffin maker in a yellow fever epidemic, he prepared to take my measure.

"What would the gentleman like? A suit of clothes in flannel or twill, perhaps?"

"Put your tape away, man! He'll take something ready-made. And I give you fair warning: Keep your shoddy for the gullible."

"As the gentleman wishes," he said in a mincing tone, which infuriated Bock.

"Horse's ass!"

The object of the captain's scorn retreated to a stool next to the handkerchiefs, where he sniffed and humphed and did his best to banish us from his thoughts.

I left, wearing a heavy duck coat, purple gabardine trousers, and a yellow flannel shirt, topped by a checked cap. The result, when I'd taken a gander of myself in the store mirror, was motley. Yet I was as pleased as I had been when graduating from knee pants to trousers.

"You look a sport! Bonaparte will be green with envy—or he would be if he weren't the color of a polished chestnut."

By now, the chestnut trees behind my house in Dobbs Ferry would have dropped their burs. The burs would have opened, and the chestnuts turned from green to brown, all ready for the roasting pan. What,

I asked myself, am I doing in Norfolk, dressed in purple pants?

22

Captain Bock owned several books on naval history and navigation. By their used condition, I guessed that he favored James Fenimore Cooper's *The History of the Navy of the United States of America*, Nathaniel Bowditch's *American Practical Navigator*, and *The Seaman's Friend*, by Richard Henry Dana, Jr., whose novel *Two Years Before the Mast* I had read at Union Seminary, when I ought to have been reading Erasmus, Luther, and Thomas Aquinas.

Before the war, I had gotten it into my head to be a parson. I had a good singing voice and took the same pleasure in belting out a hymn as "Silent Mike" Tiernan does a home run. It didn't take a chunk of shrapnel to knock the idea out of my head. No, I didn't cotton to theology, which seemed nothing more than a patchwork of contrary opinions stitched together by edict. Far from a state of grace, I felt in a state of confusion. Regulating time had been my remedy for doubt.

Books are like clocks: Time moves forward through both of them, sweeping everything before it. It's only natural that a clocksmith should admire an author's universe, which, though small, contains worlds—none better than Shakespeare's and Melville's. Not that your

154   NORMAN LOCK

stories are small potatoes, Jack. We read your reports
from the edge of existence with the same interest that
we would letters from the afterlife, hardly admitting
that we, too, will one day stop there.

As I turned the pages of *American Practical Navigator*, Bock looked on benevolently. Our Norfolk
expedition had cleared the air. Satisfied that Bonaparte and I were honest men, he would no longer keep
us at arm's length.

By that time, the *Eloise* had already traveled 370
miles from Sandy Hook. The shore was too far off
to be seen, except when the ship took advantage of
the wind and a deep-water channel closer to shore.
A headland or a bluff could sometimes be seen rising
above the ceaseless to and fro of the water as though
for the sole purpose of varying the monotony of the
view. At night, we might as well have been in mid-
ocean. Only once, during the six nights I spent aboard
the *Eloise*, did I see lights, and that was on the first
night when, unable to sleep, I went on deck. In the
dark, which would have seemed absolute but for an
ocean that appeared even blacker than the sky, I saw
a long string of lights far off to starboard. They were
bright as the Coston flares that surfmen shoot above
the sea to illuminate a foundering ship.

"It's Atlantic City," said Gus, a young sailor for
whom the novelty of a sea voyage had yet to wear off.
He was a boy, really, no more than fifteen or sixteen.

Eden's Clock   155

He was everywhere to be seen during those days and nights when we were shipmates. He would fight sleep until his head fell onto his chest. A big Polish fellow, strong as Roebling cable, would pick him lightly up and put him to bed. Gus was as excited as a boy with a Christmas box on his lap, inside of which the childish world of possibility had yet to shrink to the head of a pin on which no angels would ever dance.

"That's electric lights strung above the boardwalk. And see that twinkling that looks like stars? That's the Marlborough-Blenheim Hotel, and over there's the Traymore, sixteen stories high and topped with a gold dome! It's Moorish, don't you know. The captain told me. I never been to Atlantic City, but the captain said that one day we'll put in at the Million Dollar Pier and paint the town red, by God we will!" Gus was clearly smitten. "The captain said that if we were to run in closer to shore, we'd see HELMAR CIGARETTES spelled out in lights in the sky, like a constellation, by God we would!"

I had visited Atlantic City in the summer of 1900, during a meeting of the New York Prison Association. Zebulon Brockway, the progressive warden of Elmira Reformatory, was to speak, and nothing would do but Lilian must hear him. I rode up and down the board-walk in a rolling chair pushed by a black man, while the Holy Rollers of reform thundered against cruel and unusual punishment. They are good people—I don't mean to suggest otherwise. But they have as much chance of bringing about a just society as the religious do of making a heaven of Earth. She and I stopped for the night at a rooming house on one of the back streets, far from the electric lights.

Two nights out of Norfolk, Gus pointed to the light at Cape Hatteras, in the Outer Banks. Sweeping the coal black ocean through its Fresnel lens, the light warned mariners to keep clear of Diamond Shoals, "the graveyard of the Atlantic."

In the morning, the *Eloise* anchored in Hatteras Bight. The crew lowered the boats and rowed them through the buffeting surf to the island, where they would fill barrels from a sweet-water spring esteemed, in a former age, by the Secotan tribe, before it was laid waste by "the great mortality" smallpox brought by the goodly people of the Virginia colony. When Bock invited Bonaparte to stretch his legs onshore, he'd fingered his neck and, making a wry face, declined.

"Your friend has a great fear of hanging," said Bock as the rowers pulled for Hatteras Island. He didn't look to me for comment. The boat bounded over the waves until, with a hiss and a sigh, it slipped across the final stretch of shallow water and the prow cut into the gravelly beach.

Myrtle, pine, laurel, and oak trees pale with Spanish moss abounded on that pleasant isle. Gus picked bay leaves as earnestly as a boy does oxeye daisies, to say whether a girl loved him or loved him not. Cook would season our stews with the aromatic herb. On dry land, Gus was in his proper element. He chewed spruce gum and gamboled like a lamb. I would like to have asked why he had gone to sea. Did he have a widowed mother with too many children to feed? There are many such women, and too few Mr. Winters and Mrs. Fosters to look to their earthly needs.

I sat in the shade of a loblolly pine and listened to the sailors going about their business. Men who live beyond the pale of society have an air of villainy, comical so long as they keep their knuckle-dusters in their pockets.

"Nothing like Hatteras branch water."

"For them that care for water, maybe so."

"What's Cuba like?"

"Never been."

"This's my first trip south. I used to be an oiler on a Quebec-Philadelphia steamer."

"I went to Philadelphia once. Didn't think much of it."

"Not like New York."

"Cuba's fine for them that like rum, black beans, and green bananas."

"*Y las chicas.*"

"Sure, they're full of chili peppers."

"You bet!"

"Women are the same anyplace you go."

"Maybe in Philadelphia they are."

"New York City—now there's the place for bushwhacking!"

"And kidney cracking!"

"Get them kegs filled, you bastards, or you'll see Cuba through your arseholes!"

"Aye, aye, Admiral darling."

"Squarehead's gone sour today."

"Give a hand, Evans!"

"Righto!"

"Shorty, stick a spile in that bunghole, would you?"

"Spile your own bunghole, you bloodsucking tick!"

Bock had gone down the beach to visit one of the Outer Banks's lifesaving stations. By his account, the surfmen there were the busiest in the country and, by the number of medals and citations, the bravest. He always took them Cuban tobacco or some other treat. That day, it was his mother's plum preserves, which he'd brought from Prout's Neck.

"Stop your lollygagging," he said without much conviction as he joined us at the spring that bubbled up halfway between the Atlantic and Pamlico Sound. I could see that he'd enjoyed his visit and, like me, was feeling good under the warm Carolina sun. "Pack your horseshoes. It's time we were getting back to the *Eloise*."

The captain and I went down to the beach and

watched the sanderlings hurry on the twigs of their legs to the foaming edge of the withdrawing water. Chased to shore by a somersaulting comber, they rushed nervously onto the wet packed sand, mud crabs pinched in the black beaks of the lucky ones. Their brief avian spans are spent in advance and retreat, each a Sisyphus. One generation falls to the next, which must take up the work of survival. I wonder what time means to them, if anything at all.

The battering waves would have reminded Bock of his encounter with Winslow Homer on the beach at Prout's Neck, because he picked up the thread that he'd dropped in Norfolk: "I knew his frigid, gray, and wild ocean. Hell, I'd been looking at it ever since I was a boy. And yet I saw things in his pictures I hadn't noticed before, not as a cabin boy, an able seaman, or a third mate on a coastwise collier sailing the same piece of New England water. One picture that stuck with me he called *Northeaster*. I could taste salt in the air as the waves turned into great clouds of spray, breaking against the black ledges as the rollers came heavily against the shore. It was just a picture, Fred, but it took my breath away!"

To look upon the ocean is to see God and be damned. We are brought low, mocked, and banished to the zero hour, before the clock's first tick signaled the start of creation.

160   NORMAN LOCK

With the tip of my tongue, I touched my broken tooth.

23

Bonaparte seemed nervous and unlike his old self. (Only a writer can claim to know what sort of self that old one may have been, eh, Jack?)

WHAT'S WRONG?

"This afternoon I dreamed that I was hanged."

I pursed my lips and shook my head.

"I took it as a premonition."

He tore my scribbled reply to pieces and tossed them into the sea.

"I'm not getting off this boat till it lands in Cuba. They don't have 'niggers' there, Fred, and they don't hang black people without good reason, same as they would anyone."

That night while taking the air on deck, Bonaparte and I peered almost shyly through the dark and mist, as if an act too terrible for the naked eye were under way. How glad I would have been to see a light swinging through the blackness from a farmer's lantern, showing him the path to the barn, or from a fisherman's lamp rocking on the king post as his boat headed to sea to catch red hake! In a desolate place (none more so than an ocean at night), even misanthropes search for others of their tribe. Finding no one, they may sometimes look for God.

A CUP OF GROG WILL BUCK US UP. LET'S GO BELOW & FILCH A BOTTLE.

He kept his eyes on the pitch-black water. "Ever see a body hanged, Fred?"

I saw sorry sights in war, as well as in peace, when some drunk or madman decided that he wanted to break it. Amputations, bayonetting, men's guts spilling like sausage links, and, once, the instant when a head was blown clear off a pair of shoulders by a rebel cannonball—those I saw with my own two eyes. But not a hanging.

"I guess you weren't ever hanged, either." He kept his gaze fixed on the black ocean. "It happened to me in the Tidewater."

I laughed inwardly, not because I thought he was joking but because I knew he wasn't. The realization, awful and sudden, made me nervous and afraid, and so I had laughed to myself, as people do.

"I was a boy of six or seven or eight. I don't know, exactly, how old I was, or am. The master's son—he would've been a few years older than I was—had just come home after seeing a black man hanged in Emmerton. His father had taken him to see the fun. 'An edifying spectacle,' he called it. What my ol' master meant was a coon show without the song and dance, except for a finale of flappin' shoes. It seems a

Negro had had the gall to trip over a horse block and allow his black hand to touch a white woman. The son was all het up afterward, and nothing would do but that he must hang somebody, too. He rounded up some colored boys too young and scared to disobey. They trussed me up, got me onto a milking stool, put a noose around my neck, and, with a kick, dropped me from a rafter in the barn. The littlest one, seeing me dangle there, ran to get the master, who arrived when I was at my last gasp. He cut me down and let me fall.

"'Boy!' he shouted at his son. 'Don't you got sense enough to know the value of a slave? You ever playact with my property again, I'll beat the living hell out of you!'

"The son was sniveling, wiping snot on his sleeve, and scraping his shoes in the dust of the barn floor. He was the picture of misery and humiliation, which did my black heart good to see. Nobody appeared to notice me. I knew better than to make my presence known, abject as it was. The master of the universe—I knew no other—tossed the rope back up over the rafter and hitched another noose. I thought he meant to finish me because I was spoiled property. He turned on his boot heel and went out into the yard. In no time, he returned—I hadn't moved a muscle—with his son's dog. He hanged the poor mutt with no more thought than you'd give to hanging a ham in a smokehouse."

One way or another, we are all marked men. By

Eden's Clock   163

hanging, by war, by what is beyond what the human body can endure, we are touched and our will is forever set at naught.

There was an old man in Dobbs Ferry who kept to himself. I met him on the path beside the aqueduct when I was looking for the dog who'd gotten out of my yard. We had bought it for Louisa's enjoyment. We never saw it again. For some reason, the old man stopped me and, like Coleridge's Ancient Mariner, he fixed me with a glittering eye and said, "I held his head as we carried him across Tenth Street and into the Petersen house. 'Stand aside!' 'Give him air!' 'Clear the room!' 'Send for a doctor!' They pushed us outside. It was madness in the street. Early the next morning, Mr. Lincoln was dead, and the whole nation in mourning. After that, my life was finished, too."

Having sailed 170 miles south from Hatteras, the *Eloise* was now engaged in giving a wide berth to Frying Pan Shoals, off Bald Head Island. I do admire the ingenuity that ordinary people use in naming things; they put the efforts of poets and highfalutin advertising men to shame.

I got Bonaparte to take an interest in cards to pass the time, although the expression is hardly apt, for time seemed not to pass at all. You might say that it faltered like a child in a mire, unsure of where to put his feet.

"The banker pays Herr Heigold a double stake,"

164   NORMAN LOCK

said "Little Fritz," a Bavarian who stood at least a head taller than every other man aboard the *Eloise*. He had taught us to play skat. I liked him, though he was rarely without his mouth organ and knew only one tune.

We were playing in the stateroom that I had purchased with a watch. It was elegantly fitted, for a ship carrying Maine granite to Cuba and tobacco leaves on her return. Mr. Orville Smith must be a minor god of business to merit such luxury. The three of us sat on his bed, our boots on his emerald green sateen spread, smoking a blue streak. I hoped that our cigar smoke would get into the quilt, the pillowcases, the Oriental carpet, and the ruffled curtains, made from Javanese cloth, hung over the portlights. Let it get up the nose of Mr. Smith! I told myself. I don't begrudge him the stink.

I soon tired of the game. I have never had time for pastimes. They're a waste of spirit and of a precious commodity about which most people don't give a thought or a damn. Time began after the humiliation of Adam and Eve. Eden's clock was the first timepiece. All the clocks and watches that followed it have told the hours since the fall of man.

I went up into the pilothouse.

"Barometer's falling," said Bock, giving a fillip to the glass column of mercury.

WHERE ARE WE?

"Off Sullivan's Island and the entrance to Charleston Harbor."

HOW LONG TILL WE REACH ST. AUGUSTINE?

"Two days if the *Eloise* answers without too much back talk. Impossible to tell if we have to go bare poles. You and Bonaparte, stick to your cabin. Send up Little Fritz and the Polack. I'll need his brawn at the wheel."

24

That night, Bonaparte and I kept to the bed we shared, like Ishmael and Queequeg at the Spouter-Inn, not that there was anything cannibalistic about my bedfellow. He was a Christian, at least by affiliation with the Chapel of the Fallen, and the only tattoos I saw on him had been left on his back by a slaver's whip. I thought about Melville's novel of monomania, Ahab's for the white whale. Your stories like those in *The Son of the Wolf: Tales of the Far North* also show the littleness of men confronted by the elements. My war had been with nature of the human sort, which can be savage. I'd been one among many, a soldier in company with others who fought, fell, and, too often, died. There's comfort in being a cog in a machine, a barely noticeable part of the whole. On board the *Eloise*, I was not a part of anything, except as accident and desire had made me.

What now? Am I to be Melville's Ishmael, or your unnamed character freezing to death in Yukon Territory, or Stephen Crane's correspondent rowing for dear life in "The Open Boat"? I'm unequal to the effort needed to survive at all costs and against all odds. Some of us would rather let the water close over our heads till the door in the sea is shut. Bonaparte could survive everything, I thought, except a lynching. To show him the rope may be all it takes to choke the life out of him.

I would have slept because, when I was again on dry land, I recalled having dreamed of the boys I had seen playing in a flooded gutter. I was living in New York, at a boardinghouse on Christopher Street catering to seminarians. I had stood in the rain and watched them throwing stones at a boat made of a board and a sail cut from a shirtwaist. They seemed like three savages in their patched short trousers and middy blouses, which would, by the look of them, have been bought for a few pennies from a dealer in rags. They were intent on sinking the boat, of utterly annihilating it. If anyone could be said to be in the grip of a monomania, they were. The little scene horrified me, who was beginning to suspect that I had misheard God's call to the ministry. I didn't know what to make of their ferocity. Had I believed in hell, I'd have said that the boys were full of the devil, in the original meaning of that expression. I would

Eden's Clock 167

say now that the boat, scuppered at their childish hands, carried a cargo of their combined hatred for all those who had dropped their drawers and shat on them.

I awoke to a fearful commotion up on deck. Suddenly, the boat bucked and rose into the air, so it seemed to Bonaparte and me, who were lifted out of bed and dropped onto the cabin floor. The boat settled like a nesting hen after a shake of her feathers. An uncanny silence and calm followed, as though the world were holding its breath. In such a calm and pregnant silence did the first woman hesitate to accept the serpent's gift, while the choirs of the blessed and the army of the damned breathlessly awaited the outcome.

The *Eloise* became a creature capable of immense suffering. She shivered down her keel, which is the spine of a ship. She groaned as humans do whose bodies have been racked. How long, I asked myself, until she bursts her seams? A deck hatch blew off its hinges, and I heard a terrible roaring in my ears, such as the lion would have made when it awoke from its peaceable kingdom and leaped upon the lamb. If history had a voice, it would sound like that. Then came the crack as the mainmast splintered—the threnody that doom will trump on the last day, a noise never yet heard by living men and women. And I heard Ahab, that accursed man, shout, "Ho, ho! from all your furthest bounds, pour ye now in, ye bold billows of my whole foregone life, and top this one piled comber of my death!"

And then I drowned.

Eden's Clock 169

American Progress, John Gast, 1872

JANUARY 1906–APRIL 17, 1906

1

I HAD DROWNED IN THE SAME WAY that Bonaparte had been very nearly hanged. Like two miserable worms, we had inched into the frontier where the living confront the dead. We had not gone so far into the Rapture or the silence that we couldn't return. Not by will did we creep back into the quick of life, but by the power of something uncontrollable and aloof.

Even now, I sometimes wake from sleep or a deep slumbering state of unawareness and think, Heigold, you died on the rocks that sank the *Eloise* and sent her to the bar, to be found no longer seaworthy, and thence to the graveyard of lost ships. It's easy to believe that we are alive.

How I survived the wreck of that good ship and the loss of her crew (except Gus and the Pole, who pulled him into a lifeboat), I'll never know. Those two were carried, oarless, by the riptide far down the South Carolina coast. I learned of their escape later, when a steam packet put in at Edisto Island.

"Go on now, eat!" A black man was spooning

a peppery stew of okra and mullet into me. Boone Whaley, in whose house I awoke from my complicated transaction with death, related how the inhabitants of Edisto had lashed one another to the leeward side of fig trees at the onset of the storm that broke apart the *Eloise*, a desperate measure and last resort for the Sea Islanders, whose houses are built of tabby, a cement made of sand, ash, and crushed oyster shells fired into lime.

"What's your name, friend?" he asked kindly.

I couldn't remember my name for the space of sixty heartbeats, enough to be born again or to take a final look around the room before death overflowed its bank and swamped me.

"Can't talk?" he asked.

As I shook my head in answer, I felt resentment that I must always need to play charades. I have thoughts, the same as any other man, but a dumb one gets tired of putting words to paper or slate, like a schoolboy asked to write an essay. Not since Lilian had humbled me at the hospital in Georgetown had I indulged in self-pity, that belittling emotion that makes weaklings of us all. But you do reach a point, Jack, when you want to say "Fuck all!"

Whaley got a pencil and tore off a page from an old calendar.

FREDERICK HEIGOLD, I wrote in answer to his question.

Eden's Clock   173

That a good number of Sea Islanders can read is a credit to the northern missionaries who provided schoolhouses and teachers after the federal government deeded them property during Reconstruction. Negroes came, at last, into their own and appeared to prosper until the federal troops were withdrawn from the South and they were left all on their own to face the brutish Klan.

"Mr. Heigold, you are welcome to Edisto Island."

My guess is that he was in his fifties, well knit, if a little stooped. The whites of his eyes were clear, his teeth strong. (I beg your pardon, good man Boone, for describing you as though you were a horse.)

THERE WAS A BLACK MAN ON THE ELOISE. DO YOU KNOW WHAT BECAME OF HIM?

"Mr. Harley found him after the storm, washed up at South Creek. Mr. Harley's down from Baltimore. He paints birds. They're the dead spit of them that God made on the fifth day. Mr. Bonaparte went to fish for croakers along with Geechee Joe. They'll be back before long."

Half asleep, I heard Boone tell the story of my own deliverance.

"When the storm blew out, we went down and saw pieces of ship on the sand. Lillie May shouted for us to look at the gnashing teeth of the ocean as it pulled back its lips to spit you out, like Jonah, through its gaping mouth, onto dry land. We carried you here

174   NORMAN LOCK

to my house, thinking you were dead. It seemed like you had gone into your own ocean. Cotto came by with . . ."

I heard no more, having fallen asleep.

Lilian, her suddenly inert body, makes a sound exactly as if a half-empty sack of meal fell on the floor. I put down the book I am reading and rush to the foot of the stairs. "Lilian!" I say, and I do not think it the least strange that I can talk. But now it is for her to be silent.

A sharp goose quill poking through the pillow brought me to my senses. I was alone in the room, with only the spicy odor of fish stew to confirm my memory of having eaten and of someone's having fed me—a man whose teeth are strong.

On a caned chair beside the bed were sun-bleached cotton trousers and a shirt. I did not yet believe that a revelation could be had by a change of clothes. Heigold would be Heigold, no matter in whose shoes he walked.

2

That evening, Bonaparte and I walked on a broad beach raked by light from the westering sun. Soon, the ocean would turn to gold, and gulls row through deepening air toward the mangroves, voicing their sardonic opinion of humankind. In the abrupt fall of the easterlies, a silence would open, in which waves,

Eden's Clock   175

tripping and foaming over the pebbled shore, would seethe. Night would come like a scythe, and the long shadows of the cypress trees would disappear.

"Four hundred tons of ship and stone and not a ripple left!" said Bonaparte. "A newly made grave ought to leave a scar."

In his cry, I heard, again, the torment of the *Eloise* caught in the iron grip of a sea gone mad with fury against all human enterprises, whether a three-masted schooner built by Arthur Sewall & Company or the Gullah Geechees' flimsy houses, which, the imperial ocean would remind them, belong to it, just as those who live in them had belonged to cotton planters and Eli Whitney's cotton gin.

WHAT HAPPENED TO CAPTAIN BOCK?

"Drowned, most likely. He was in the pilothouse when the *Eloise* keeled over."

THE OTHERS?

"I saw two boats lowered."

AND?

He lifted his hands, then let them fall. From that gesture, I understood, maybe for the first time, that every man and woman can be left speechless by an occasion that beggars language. It is a humiliation common to us all.

Boone Whaley joined us at the water's edge. He brought corncob pipes and a pouch of homegrown tobacco. The Gullah people make their livings selling tobacco, cotton, okra, indigo, and rice to the whites on the "other side," their name for the South Carolina mainland that lies across a wide marshland threaded by tidal streams.

The strong tobacco made me cough. Boone and Bonaparte clapped me on the back and laughed like two conspirators. Did they see me as a white man, with a white man's follies? I no longer saw them as black. I take that back. Never for a moment did I see them as anything else, with my white man's eyes. Maybe that's as it should be: To ignore their color is to make them invisible, to erase what is undeniable, to rob them of what belongs to them—a theft not so very different from changing a man's name from Abu Abioseh of Sierra Leone to George Washington Jarvis, property of Randolph P. Jarvis of Memphis, Tennessee. How Lilian used to rage against such high-handedness, which she said was "no better than stealing Florida from the Seminoles!"

The tide was well up, although still at the flood, which flattened the eelgrass. Under the moon, the Atlantic was pale, smooth, and phosphorescent. Only the hissing surf, the noise of the reedbirds, and the occasional splash of a heavy fish breaching the surface of the water disturbed the silence. The cedar trees leaned in, as if to hear the unspoken.

3

I tramped the island's sand roads, angled for drum, mullet, and redfish, caught blue crabs, and visited Geechee families. To eyes like mine that retained an image of time's ruthless progress seen, in miniature, in the secret life of clocks, their lives seemed becalmed. They tended the fields, orchards, and burial plots of their ancestors, fished from the beach or a boat, mended nets, pots, roofs, and clothing, went to the praise house, and raised their voices in raucous song and shouts to a god that resembled mine but also those of West Africa, such as *kan-imba*, meaning "endless space." Endless space and time belonged to them; that is how it seemed to me, who never, in nearly three months on Edisto, saw anyone die. (One man would die by another's hand, but both men were white and only passing through.)

I remember standing beside Geechee Sam on a mud bank of Ocella Creek, across from Fig Island. A basket woven of bulrushes, like that which had carried the infant Moses down the Nile, had been lowered into the turbid water. Sam had baited the trap with a spoiled chicken leg tied to its bottom. The tide was coming in fast, and the blue crabs would be crazed by the scent of putrid meat, a sorry fact that proves the allure of corruption. The drowned black man who had

178   NORMAN LOCK

seen me off at Dobbs Ferry, in a manner of speaking, came to mind, and with him Captain Bock. Must he swim the waters of the world until he fetches up at Tarrytown or Shanghai, Milwaukee or Rotterdam, Savannah or Sevastopol? What time will the gold Patek Philippe, with its twelve complications, keep— common, supernal, or none at all? Will it measure the pace of snails and glaciers or tick backward to the second day, when the firmament was divided into the waters below and those above? Imagination is not an exclusive faculty of poets; mechanics possess it also.

"You look like you left yourself someplace, Mr. Fred," said Sam, eyeing me sidewise.

Maybe I did. Maybe I'm on the *Eloise*, or what's left of her. Maybe I'm down underneath the mud, hoping that I'll be overlooked in the final accounting of my race.

"Want I should pick you some figs?"

I shook my head, wishing that I could shake off the feeling of dismemberment. At Union Hospital as I waited for my throat to heal, I overheard a number of soldiers struggle to describe the sensation of having lost an arm or a leg. None could put it into words. Had I the tongue of an angel, I could not have done so, either. For all their eloquence, Walt Whitman and Louisa May Alcott, who ministered to the wounded and the dying at that hospital, would have

Eden's Clock   179

been stumped for words. Only the maimed have the right to speak of maiming.

Eat some figs, Heigold, or get Lillie May to brew a pot of dandelion and burdock tea.

Not every ill can be cured, nor every hurt healed. Simples are just that and not much use against complexity.

"Do you think you'll stay awhile?" asked Sam. He held a line tied to the unseen chicken part. When the crabs tore into it, the music of ravenous hunger would sound along its length. It is one of the chords played by our lower nature, which the world miscalls "bestial." It stretches all the way to the stars.

What were my plans? It took a moment to remember what had brought me a thousand miles south of Dobbs Ferry.

I'M GOING TO SAN FRANCISCO.

Sam chuckled. "You sure been taking the dog's own leg!"

ONE THING OR ANOTHER HAS PUT ME OFF THE TRACK.

For months, I had been on my way to the Pacific, only to have gone no farther than the South Carolina coast.

"What's that place got, you have to turn the world upside down to get there?"

I had not even a shrug of an answer to give him.

He looked at me, as at a curious specimen washed

180   NORMAN LOCK

up on the beach, which I suppose I was. "You've got the stares is what I think."

STARES?

"Your eyes get stuck on something, so's you can't look away."

I had come down with listlessness, hard to shake off—yes, a staring into space, as Sam thought of it. Maybe I'd been ensnared by *kan-imba*. Would I have the strength to leave this Calypso's cave or, like Odysseus on his return to Ithaca from Troy, languish for seven years?

"I can carry you upriver to some folks who'll get you to the Savannah train," said Sam, as if he had read my thoughts. (My mind has a voice of its own, chockfull of fine words and figures of speech, which come naturally to a person whose head is so often bowed over a book.)

I went home. By then, the world had shrunk to the island and my notion of home to the empty rice loft where I slept. Its walls were covered with newspaper; the Sea Islanders believe that hags and haints must read every word of print set in front of them before they can work their mischief. As if I myself were an evil spirit whose eyes were caught on the barbs of type, I read a summary of events published in the January 16, 1878, edition of the Abbeville, South Carolina, *Press and Banner*:

January 17: House of Representatives held Louisiana Returning Board in contempt . . . **26:** Electoral Commission bill passed by Congress . . . **30:** Both Houses of Congress chose members of Electoral Commission . . . **31:** Electoral Commission organized . . . **February 1:** Electoral count commenced . . . **5:** Steamer *George Washington* sank off Cape Race; twenty-five lives lost . . . **11:** Egyptian troops defeated by Abyssinians . . . **15:** Attempt made to assassinate Governor Packard . . . **16:** Steamer *George Cromwell* wrecked; thirty lives lost . . . **31:** Three schooners wrecked off Long Island; eleven men drowned . . . **March 2:** Result of electoral count announced in Congress . . . **19:** Disturbances in New Orleans between Nicholls and Packard factions . . . **21:** President Hayes sent a special commission to Louisiana . . . **April 6:** Spotted Tail surrendered . . . **10:** Troops withdrawn from Columbia, S.C. . . . **17:** Boss Tweed confessed . . . **19:** Nicholls faction gained possession of Louisiana state government . . . **20:** Troops withdrawn from New Orleans . . . **24:** Czar declares war on Turkey; Russian troops crossed into Romania . . . **June 21:** Eleven Mollie Maguires executed

182 NORMAN LOCK

in Pennsylvania . . . **July 1:** 60,000 Russian troops crossed the Danube at Sistova . . . **3:** Wells and Anderson of Louisiana Returning Board indicted . . . **11:** Seven workmen suffocated by gas in a coal mine at Brookfield, Penna. . . . **15:** General Howard fought Nez Perces . . . **16:** Russians captured Nikopolis . . . **17:** Baltimore and Ohio Railroad strike . . . **20:** Riot in Baltimore; troops fired into crowd, killing eight . . . **22:** Many lives and millions of dollars in property lost in Pittsburgh riot; U.S. troops sent to scenes of disturbances . . . **25:** Rioters and police skirmished in Chicago . . . **August 1:** Troops fired on mob at Scranton, Penna., killing four . . . **11:** General Gibbon fought Nez Perces in Montana . . . **18:** Two satellites of the planet Mars discovered . . . **September 5:** Crazy Horse captured and killed . . . .

By what sleights of hand and devious ways a column of tawny newsprint composed and printed two hundred miles inland and twenty-eight years earlier happened to be pasted to a wall on an island in the Atlantic, a clocksmith from Dobbs Ferry could not explain.

4

Walking on the beach that night, Bonaparte and I smoked strong Edisto-grown tobacco, which no longer scalded my throat. Before the light had gone out of the sky, I tried to convey the torpor that had taken hold of me to Bonaparte, who had become fluent in the language of the mute.

"I feel it, too," he said. "Like I ate the lotus. One moment I tell myself, It's time to go; the next, Why not stay awhile longer? It's good here. Then my neck will get to itching, and I wonder how long before a cracker decides to string up the Yankee coon who has the gall to live across the marsh from him."

A wave slapped the beach hard enough to startle us, scatter the sanderlings, and ignite the atoms of phosphorescence tumbling in the ocean's churn.

"The other night I saw Captain Bock."

I pulled Bonaparte's sleeve, wanting to hear more.

"Cold fire was leaking from his clothes. Otherwise, he looked as he did before."

I pulled his sleeve insistently.

"He didn't have anything much to say for himself, if that's what you want to know. But I sensed his thoughts, as sometimes I do yours. He warned us not to get stuck here like barnacles on a piling. It's time to get off this beach, Fred! Mr. Winter used to tell his congregation, 'Get off your duffs before it's too late, you sitters of park benches, stoops, and stumps! You wallflowers! The worst sin is to sit out your life and let someone else take your place at the ball.' Nobody paid him any mind. I've made up mine to go down to Hilton Head and get on the first boat bound for Cuba."

Turning my pockets inside out, I cocked my head like a curious owl.

"I've enough to get started. I've been planting beans and okra ever since the last frost of the year. If I run out of money, I'll play cards. If I run out of luck, I'll jump overboard and swim. I've been to the ball; I know how to dance to every sort of fiddle."

With gestures that he may not have seen in the deep darkness under a loblolly pine where we'd stopped, I acknowledged his decision and my sadness that we would be parting. I'd grown fond of Bonaparte. Still, I had known the day would come. And what business had I in Cuba?

The acute sensitivity to the invisible strings that bind us, one to another, the living to the dead, the sighted to the blind, the hearing to the deaf, the talkative to the dumb, which sometimes takes hold of us, would have taken hold of my friend, since he replied to my unspoken question by saying, "I'm leaving the day after tomorrow."

I wished that time would stand still the way the

sun and moon had done for Joshua. But the juggernaut rolls over us all.

5

The blind man mended fishing nets in a shed built behind the house, where he lived with his son and daughter-in-law. While I was on Edisto, I never heard him called by a proper name; he was always "the blind man." Like Tiresias, the sightless seer, he was sought by those with troubling dreams. Bonaparte visited his shed after seeing Captain Bock shining like fox fire on the beach. I went along with him.

"I don't know what it means," the blind man told him, sitting cross-legged on the floor of his house, mending shuttle in one hand, thread in the other. I had a feeling that he saw something visible only to his kind.

Bonaparte asked him what he was looking at with his dead eyes fixed on the far away.

"Nothing."

His reply was unsatisfactory, his manner flip. But how could a mute man rebuke a blind one?

"That's all?" asked Bonaparte, his voice wavering between disappointment and mistrust.

"Nothing is not empty." His voice was not oracular. He was not the "Poughkeepsie Seer" reincarnated as a black man on a South Carolina barrier island. If anything, he sounded annoyed.

"What's there to fill it?" asked Bonaparte a little defiantly.

"*Kan-imba.*"

"Does *kan-imba* have a word for me?"

"He does not speak."

"Ah! Like my friend here, whom you can't see."

"I see him well enough."

The man's son came into the shed and asked if Bonaparte and I would take a mended net to Geechee Sam, who kept his mullet skiff at Big Bay Creek. Having been put off by the father's reticence, Bonaparte muttered that he'd be damned if he would. In the dooryard, an anthill had been raised beside the path. He demolished it in a sudden fury, whose cause, I thought, must be something other than irritation. I imagined the ants inside the ruin, their home of crumbled earth transformed into a burial mound.

I offered to take the net to Sam.

He was not at the creek. I left the net in his boat and leaned against the gunwale. The salt hay whispered to the tide's change. I rolled a cigarette, my heavy shoes stamping the outline of their soles into cold mud.

I picked up a bog turtle and held it along its bony edge. The green head flinched into its pleated neck. By the laying on of hands did I confer our notion

Eden's Clock   187

of time on the frightened animal, or, perchance, did my heartbeat come nearly to a stop in the sluggish way of reptiles? Crabs and other creatures that escape inclemency in torpor would be stirring soon, along with the roots of dune grass, pennywort, and morning glories, as April came up from the deeper South and settled on the Carolina coast. The air would become fragrant with magnolia and jasmine, the live oaks green.

Lillie May called Edisto Island "Canaan Land," which, as the Lord said to Moses, "is the land that shall fall unto you for an inheritance, even the land of Canaan with the coasts thereof." The River Jordan flowed through the Sea Islands, and the Gullah forefathers, unseen and unheard by me, fished for flounder, red drum, kingfish, and mullet as they smoked fat cigars.

Fool that I was, I could not see the truth of those around me, whose black bodies may have borne the scars of slavers' whips or whose memories, gotten by hard living or by legacy, held the westward exodus into the interior at the start of the war and, at the end of it, in the rear of Sherman's burning march through Georgia, on their weary, footsore return to Edisto Island. Nor did I read in their gnarled hands, stooped backs, and faces deeply lined from scrabbling for their daily bread the crushing weight of human toil. I, too, it seems, was just passing through.

188   NORMAN LOCK

All along, I had believed a clock to be an instrument by which time is kept and, being so, kept in check. But at that moment, with the smell of decomposition making my nose twitch, I realized that a clock stands between us and time like a screen thrown hastily around a hospital bed, when nothing more can be done for some poor mortal's mortal part.

6

While on Edisto Island, I barely seemed to touch ground. I got my hands dirty enough, stuck in the earth and in the guts of fish. My boots were caked in mud and manure. But I floated, as much a ghost as Captain Bock and as absent a presence as Bonaparte, who had left for Cuba, where his color would not count against him. Or so he hoped.

Often after I had eaten a porridge of sea oats or rice, along with fried corn cakes and cups of chicory coffee, I sought the company of Sipio Bass, who could be found at the burying place, behind the praise house, which he tended with reverence and curses. Eighty years old and often confused, he claimed almost everybody buried there as kith or kin. His mind had turned back its clock. I listened to him talk to the air, to the dead, to the grass growing on top of them.

I would take him an offering from my world to

his: a chestnut, a yellow pebble from a gravel wash, a sunflower, seeds pecked out of its mummified head by blue-green parakeets, some camphor weed, a honeycomb, or a wild ginger root. He would accept each gift without acknowledgment, sniff it, consider its qualities, judge its suitability, and place it on a gravestone. If I brought corn whiskey, he would pour most of it on the ground to appease the haints, then drink what was left. He paid me no mind; I might have been one of them, plotting mischief.

Mr. Harley, the artist from Baltimore, Maryland, also comes into the story. Now and then, I would accompany him to the salt meadow, in search of birds to sketch. I expect that he appreciated me both as an eager listener and a silent one. He had refused to go into the family business, a shirt-collar concern in Baltimore. Young Harley wanted nothing to do with collars, "Albany, Piccadilly, or butterfly." He made a living selling his watercolors to card and calendar printers. Once, he'd had an exhibition of his oils in Savannah. He was devoted to painting and passionate about the birds themselves. Snowy egrets, brown pelicans, blue herons, purple grackles—Harley mourned the violent undoing of their creation by milliners and their women customers who must sport a dead bird on their hats.

"After God said, 'Let there be this' and 'Let there be that,' He left the world to roll on, on its own. I tell you, Heigold, the human race would be damned lucky to have descended from the monkeys, as Darwin has it, instead of a pair of complacent do-nothings!" He was bitter for such a young man. "Want to know the first thing Eve did when she was thrown out of Eden? Kill a bird of paradise to make a hat with."

Harley boiled as he spoke of a run-in with a bird hunter named Rollins. Harley had been sketching, in pastels, a black oystercatcher, its beak a dazzling vermilion, nesting on the beach above the tidal mark. Unobserved by the artist, who was intent on his sketch, the hunter stole within a dozen paces of the bird. He shot it, and while Harley stood there flat-footed, he put it in his bag.

"I apologize for the interruption."

"The bastard smirked!" said Harley. "I saw red and went at him with a fool crayon in my hand! I wasn't worth swatting. If only he hadn't smirked! I swear I'll shoot him dead if I get the chance!"

7

In Boone Whaley's barn, I found the corpse of a Chippendale tall clock, built by Simon Willard at the end of the eighteenth century, in Roxbury, Massachusetts. Its mahogany case had turned leprous in the Sea Island salt air; the brass and ball finials had tarnished. The Boston fretwork above the bonnet was

Eden's Clock 191

broken. Six months earlier, I'd have put on mourning for the wreck of so fine a work of art.

HOW DID YOU COME BY THIS?

"My grandfather found it on Kiawah Beach," replied Boone, intent on the clock face, as though its hands might start to move again. "The waves set it down on the beach, like a mother lifting her baby out of the tub. Along with some broken chairs, it was all that was left after the *Savannah* broke apart on the reef. Grandfather took it, according to the law of salvage. It was left to my father and came down to me. God must have cursed me, since it hasn't told time since my seekin'. When I was small, I'd watch the moon painted on the dial go through its phases." Boone took a rag from his back pocket and wiped the dust from the inlays. "It stood in the kitchen till I got a new coal stove; then I brought it out here. Lillie May is all the time telling me to get rid of it, a broken clock. 'What good is it?' she asks. 'And it might bring bad luck, besides.' I tell her, 'God knows what mischief would've come to us if I'd chopped it up for kindling.' So I polish it with beeswax and keep it in the barn."

I opened the bonnet. There was sand in the teeth of the gears. I closed it. I had no tools to fix it. And who knows whether or not the island might be better without it? Since being among the Gullah, I'd become superstitious. I'd never gone inside the praise house,

192   NORMAN LOCK

but I'd heard the people shout and beat sticks on the floor as they shambled in a ring, performing a dance that made me feel giddy just listening to it.

We went into the kitchen, and Boone cooked me some red rice and pork on the stove.

"I'll miss your bony white ass," he said. "The people say you have a good soul. They say you don't bring shame on your ancestors, who probably had bony white asses, too. They say you're welcome here, if you come back. Send us a picture of the Pacific Ocean, and say whether or not it be blue."

Lillie May gave me sea-oat bread, dried red peas, a smoked fish, and a blue glass bottle of spring-water— all in a coiled sweetgrass basket. She gave me fennel seeds to chew and an *ibiri*, made of dried palm leaves, a totem sacred to Nana Buluku, who lives near muddy places and governs the dead. I slipped it into my pocket and kissed Lillie May's cheek. She patted mine, her palm inscribed with enough lines to confound a chirologist.

"Let's go, Fred!" said Sam, embarrassed by the fuss of departure. He would take me up the Edisto River, aboard his mullet skiff, as far as Fenwick Cut.

I took a last look at my Gullah saviors standing before their house, which Boone Whaley had painted "haint blue," the color of a Sea Island sky, to make it invisible to haunts and hags.

8

I felt the narrow river pass through my hand as I worked the tiller and Sam rowed. The muscles of his shoulders knotted and unknotted like hawsers. The air was spiced by marsh mud, myrtle, dog fennel, mullein, and beach plum, whose purple fruit had turned to jam, to the delight of the ecstatic bees. The black water being low in the channel, I couldn't see above the reeds' tasseled heads. On the Sea Island, my eyes had become used to distant vantages. On that river, there was none, and the muscles of my eyes grew cramped like those of my legs. There was nothing to see but the golden palisades of reeds, skirted with mud. The sky narrowed above me; it held neither cloud, bird, nor harbinger. The feeling of submersion returned and, with it, panic.

Sam may have sensed my distress. He asked if I'd heard the news about Mr. Harley, to take my mind away.

I gave him a practiced look of inquiry. (A mute has a repertoire of gestures suitable to every occasion.)

"He shot the bird catcher. Killed him stone dead."

I motioned for Sam to tell me more.

"The Rockville sheriff and deputies from the other side are hunting him. I feel sorry for Mr. Harley. It was a good thing he done."

Harley had told me, "One thousand six hundred and eight packages of heron plumes were auctioned in a single day at a London commercial trading house. At thirty ounces a package, that's 48,240 ounces. It takes four birds for an ounce of plumes; therefore, 192,960 great white herons were slaughtered and sold to decorate ladies' hats. Plume hunters get thirty-two dollars an ounce. With so much money at stake, men like that will cut your throat and pull your molars for watch fobs if you get in their way."

Sam put me ashore at Fenwick Island, where his brother and nephew farmed indigo and okra. I passed three days in fitful travel by wagon, buggy, and boat as my Negro conductors moved me northward, like a runaway in whiteface or an article of contraband—first to Walls Cut, then Jehossee Island, and finally Willtown Bluff, where I boarded a Seaboard Air Line Railroad train to Savannah. My benefactors asked nothing in return, but they accepted my help in the field or kitchen with gratitude, as people do who know the value of labor and self-worth.

On the train ride, a bird flew into the car from the vestibule. You'd have thought it was a turkey vulture by the way the people carried on. The men whooped and waved their hats at what was only a common wren. I felt sorry for it, hearing it screech and churr as it flapped against the car windows, wanting to get out. At last, it settled on a woman, who had the sense

Eden's Clock   195

to keep still, until it caught its wings in the netting of her hat, next to a stuffed white-bellied swallow and a pile of wax cherries.

I thought of painter Harley. I hoped the sheriff and his posse wouldn't catch him. The devil take all poachers, hat trimmers, and silly women who like to wear dead things on their heads.

9

In Savannah, I went into the depot lunchroom, and there, over a slice of pecan pie and a cup of coffee, I fell into conversation with a man from St. Louis.

"Do you have a moment, friend?" he asked as he sidled into a chair opposite me and put his bag beneath the table.

I HAVE NO TIME, EXCEPT AS IT PLEASES THE RAILWAY.

"What I have to show you will not only astonish but may also arouse a covetousness, a desire to possess, that you may never have thought was part of your character."

I felt my eyes glaze over as they will when a pitchman or a preacher starts in on you.

"Friend, you have every right to be skeptical. If I were in your shoes"—his were tan, the pointy toes stained by tobacco spittle—"I would be, likewise."

The lucky juju given me by an Edisto root doctor

196   NORMAN LOCK

was proving useless against the spiel of this modern brand of haint. (What potency can there be in a strip of newsprint carried in one's shoe?)

"Like I always say, 'If it don't pan, it's black sand. If it don't wash, it's a load of crap.'" He hardly stopped to draw breath. "I'm from Missouri, the 'Show Me' state. I'm so cautious, I believe I could trace my ancestors back to Joseph of Arimathea's garden, where Thomas the Great Doubter disbelieved in the wounds held up for his inspection by the Lord Jesus Christ!"

I looked around the lunchroom to see what effect the shyster's words were having on the drummers dressed in flashy suits, stout matrons tugging at their corsets, harried mothers beset by troublesome offspring, and businessmen wearing black, as though in mourning for their futures in wheat. No one took the slightest interest in my interlocutor's palaver.

WHAT DO YOU HAVE TO SHOW ME?

He put his palms together, laced the fingers, and intoned like a parson, "Ah! How often have I seen cynicism and curiosity go hand in hand!"

My irritation would have been plain to see, and he hurriedly got to the point. Dropping his voice to a whisper, he said, "Behold!" From his carpetbag, he produced a thighbone.

Scratching a mosquito bite on the back of my neck, I looked at the bone and then at him. "It belonged to none other than Abraham Lincoln!" He pushed back his derby, opened his coat, and fingered the buttons of his houndstooth vest.

I was about to show my backside to the gouger, when he grabbed my hand, as if he meant to snap it from my wrist and put it in his reliquary bag to sell to a gullible rube up the line as the hand that held the pistol that killed Jesse James. His fingers may have been those of an expert at cards and an escort of rich women, slender and immaculate, but there was nothing delicate about that grip.

"You are wondering how this relic—for it belonged to America's only martyred saint—came to be in my possession."

He let go of my hand. Rubbing my wrist, I eased into the chair, and with the magnanimity of a bishop, I gestured that I would hear him out.

"You will have heard of 'Big Jim' Kennally." He looked at me for confirmation, which I withheld. "In the seventies, Big Jim was an Illinois wholesaler, a middleman between 'shovers' and counterfeiters. In '75, Secret Service agents collared Ben Boyd, probably the finest engraver of bogus notes in the country. With Ben in the pen, supply went dry as the Mojave. That's when Big Jim conceived one of the boldest, most daring plots in the history of kidnap and ransom.

"On Election Day of 1876, Big Jim and his gang of cutthroats planned to break into the Lincoln mausoleum at Oak Ridge Cemetery, stuff the body in a

198   NORMAN LOCK

sack, and take it by wagon from Springfield to northern Indiana, where they would bury it in a sand dune near Lake Michigan. There it would remain until Ben was put back into circulation and Big Jim got richer, to the tune of fifty grand. The plot was foiled by a Secret Service 'roper' named Lewis Swegles, parttime merchant seaman, part-time petty crook, and part-time police informant. Ten days after Big Jim and his bone rustlers had shot their way out of the cemetery, lawmen cornered them in Chicago." The Missourian's voice sank to pianissimo. Soon it would be audible only to dogs. "Big Jim got nabbed, but not before selling several ivories belonging to the former president to a fence, whose name I can't divulge without putting myself at risk. Big Jim won a year in Jolliet, the maximum sentence for grave robbing in Illinois at the time. This here remnant of Mr. Lincoln's carcass fell into my lap by a lucky accident. I'm not at liberty to say any more about it."

The con man from St. Louis—I never caught his name—spun one hell of a yarn, Jack, and I bestowed on him an expression signifying appreciation, as I would have on an organ grinder's monkey that had danced a jig. He mistook it as a sign that he had overcome all resistance in his mark.

"Mister, I'll be frank, though it makes me look an awful chump." He jerked his head from side to side to deter eavesdroppers, leaned toward me, and spoke

Eden's Clock 199

behind his hand. "In my youth, I studied anthropology at the University of Missouri. My life would be very different but for a fondness for games of chance." He hung his head on his fancy vest, the picture of remorse. "I was on my way to assist the eminent paleontologist Edward Drinker Cope in the exhumation of dinosaur remains at Como Bluff, Wyoming. Yesterday, I lost my traveling money in a game of faro." He dropped his voice further to signify that he would not care for his improvidence to become common knowledge.

I had read about Cope in the Albany papers published at the time of his death, in 1897. "I'm forced to sell this magnificent thighbone of the Great Emancipator. What would you say to twenty dollars?" He would have noticed the shaping of a refusal in the muscles of my face, because he quickly lowered the price to ten.

He went so far as to place my pencil in my hand, jerking his head toward the notebook, and urging me to bargain.

"If there remains a shred of doubt concerning the merchandise, I'll have Dr. Charles De Costa Brown attest to its authenticity. It was he who embalmed the body of the slain president and then traveled with the coffin from Washington to Springfield, Missouri, to apply paint and powder to the corpse during the thirteen-day train trip. I'm told that the air inside the parlor car was ripe. Retired from the affairs of men, Dr. Brown lives quietly not far from this spot. We can be there and back before your train departs."

I had read Dr. Brown's obituary in the papers, as well. He died the year before Dr. Cope.

I looked out the lunchroom window. The locomotive was getting up the necessary steam to depart. I opened my wallet and showed him its contents: a two-dollar bill. (In my right shoe, I kept the rest of my money, a more efficacious talisman than the strip of newspaper in the other.)

His face fell, he scratched his cheek, and pulled at an ear. "For two dollars, I can let you have Mr. Lincoln's nose."

I boarded the train as the locomotive's iron lungs blew smoke and cinders into the warm Savannah afternoon, leaving the purveyor of bones of doubtful origin in the railway lunchroom, decorated by a garish chromolithograph of *Custer's Last Fight*, commissioned by Anheuser-Busch. The mosquito bite on my neck was giving me fits.

10

I took sick with fever and was put off the train before my trip west could be said to have begun. Reeling in the sun, I was helped into the back of a farmer's wagon, or so I believed it to be in my delirium.

Eden's Clock 201

A boy sits beside me, eating raw corn. He has no flesh on his bones to speak of. He tells me that until four weeks ago he was a New York guttersnipe. A month in Canaan Land has not been long enough to fatten him after a diet of leavings in the Tenderloin. He wears the raiment bestowed on each boy by the Children's Aid Society before making his western debut. His has been a failure on account of his teeth. One of a number of boys who has been packed off to green pastures, he was stood up in front of a crowd as though to be auctioned or shot. His swollen jaw betrayed him. On closer inspection, aided by fingers of dubious cleanliness, two dog's teeth were found to be rotted. The boy, whose name is Michael Nolan, got passed over and would have been put aboard the orphan train and sent up the line to another town, by the Tacoma method, if not for a rube and his wife, who agreed to take him.

"They loaded me into the back of their buckboard, along with sacks of feed and potatoes. We rode out a long way into the country, which was flat and mostly planted in corn, with here and there a clump of trees. I didn't care for it and missed New York and the rowdies I pigged with who hadn't got caught by missionaries and such. They were always going on about the city being no fit place for children living all mixed up together like a litter of mutts. I'd gone along for the new duds they gave me and to get rid of the scabies."

"Did the rube and his wife treat you well?"

"They only hurt me the once when they yanked out my

teeth. I expect a real tooth puller couldn't have done better, 'less he dumbed me with whiskey. Being Holy Rollers, they didn't keep strong drink in the house or the barn, either. They prayed at me like a pair of butchers sawing off a hog's head. They'd get me up the middle of the night and have a go at me, first one, then the other. When they took to dunking my head in a tub of ice water, I knew I had to get the hell away from there before I got pneumonia and died."

"*So you ran off?*" He nodded in the affirmative.

"*You can come with me,*" I tell him.

"*Which way you headed?*"

"*To San Francisco.*"

"*That's west, ain't it?*"

"*It is.*"

"*Thanks just the same, mister, but I'm fed up with the West.*" He points to the distant hills. "*East?*" he asks.

"*Yes.*"

"*I'll be on my way, then.*" *He gets ready to climb down from the wagon. I take hold of his shirttail and gesture that he should wait. I bring out the basket that Lillie May gave me on Edisto Island, containing sea-oat bread, a salt fish, red rice, and a bottle of water, all of which has been miraculously replenished, like the stone jug at the wedding in Cana. I watch the boy walk toward "the hills of silence, which are beyond the edge of the earth."*

Your words, Jack.

It started to rain.

I opened my eyes. A woman was bathing me with

Eden's Clock   203

a sponge. As I got used to the light coming in at the window, I saw that she was wearing a nurse's cap and apron. The water was cool and smelled of witch hazel.

"Lilian!" I thought I was back in Georgetown, don't you see. But the word, the sound of it, had died in my throat, like water poured on sand.

"Welcome to the land of the living," she said as she lifted my arm to wash my armpit. "I could have lit a match on your forehead! You should feel better now that the fever broke."

11

Well enough to travel, I took an East Tennessee Railway train bound for Memphis. By then, I had seen too much scenery to take an interest in what passed outside the window like a moving-picture show. To give an account of the trains I rode and the railways I traveled on would be tedious, Jack. Suffice it to say that I spent five days crossing the country, sleeping, stretching my legs at whistle-stops along the way, eating in depot lunchrooms, reading a dog-eared copy of *The Children of the Frost*, which someone had left at the contagious hospital, and listening to strangers. I used to think that we are nothing but our stories; now I say that we are nothing but a walking digest of other people's tales. I'll tell you some I overheard as I made my westward progress.

"I wonder if you'd let me sit by the window. I notice that you don't look outside. This is my first time this far west. I lived all my life in Pittsburgh, Pennsylvania. An awful town, to tell the truth, the air always full of soot. You can't hang wash outside to dry without it getting dirty. I was glad to leave, though it took the house falling down around my ears. Every so often, a house will get swallowed up by a coal mine underneath. My mother and father and my brother, Ned, went with it. I was at the grocer's. I'm going to stay with my aunt in Oakland."

I agreed that she should have my seat. She looked to be sixteen or seventeen. To have lost her family, house, and place in the world (no matter how grim and sooty) at so young an age and at a single stroke—hers was no common bereavement. Yet she was cheerful as she spoke about a new life in California. She was a lively, audacious young person given to making pert remarks about the other passengers, which were in no way cruel. Nor was she the least embarrassed, as some people are, to carry on a conversation with a mute.

WILL YOU FIND SOME WORK TO DO THERE—OR ENROLL IN A NORMAL SCHOOL OR ONE OF THE SECRETARIAL BUREAUS? WOULD YOU LIKE TO WORK IN AN OFFICE?

"I don't know about school. . . . A job, I think,

Eden's Clock   205

is what I want. In Pittsburgh, I worked for Woolworth's, at the notions counter. I was happy there. I stood near where they roasted cashews and peanuts. It was wonderful."

I thought it must be, to hear her tell it.

Behind me, two women had been talking about church socials, baking bread, picnics, children, and grandchildren, until their voices faded into a single wordless drone. My eyes glazed with the recollection of a trout stream in Peekskill, where I had lay me down to sleep amid the fragrance of sweet alyssum and the humming of bees that paid me no mind. I would have soon drifted into another sleep, if not for a story one of the women began to tell the other about the two Murphy brothers taken in by a farmer named Hardesty after their mother and father died in a house fire in town. He put them to work cutting asparagus because they were "low to the ground." Chas, the younger boy, died of a fever. Hardesty buried him on his place; Michael Murphy dug the hole. One day the farmer took a strap to him. When he turned his back, Michael stuck a pitchfork in him so forcefully that the sheriff had to struggle to remove it. The sheriff later said that the boy must have had the strength of a grown man's hatred in him.

206   NORMAN LOCK

The boy ran, was caught, and was sent to Menard Penitentiary for fifteen years.

The tale would make a stone weep, if not a righteous man who sits a pew every Sunday and votes the straight Republican ticket.

I could make out enough of the words to understand that he was praying. I kept my eyes shut. To discuss God's goodness or man's sinful nature would have put a strain on the resources of pencil and paper. Three times the old man had muttered the words of the prayer before I remembered it in its entirety: "Almighty and everlasting God, who hatest nothing that Thou hast made and dost forgive the sins of all them that are penitent, create and make in us new and contrite hearts, that we, worthily lamenting our sins and acknowledging our wretchedness, may obtain of Thee, the God of all mercy, perfect remission and forgiveness." Long ago, I had listened to the chaplain speak them, ardently and fearfully, after stumbling over the body of a Confederate infantryman who, unclaimed and unburied, had been left in the field to rot.

White fluffs of cottonwood clung to the shoulders of the man sitting beside me, as if he had walked beneath a tree branch heavy with new snow.

Eden's Clock   207

I couldn't see her face; she hid it behind a veil. When she spoke, the words came from behind it, fluttering the black tulle. I could not have told you the shape of her mouth or the color of her eyes. She would have been at least fifty, because she told me that she'd met her husband in the summer of 1874, at an Independence Day picnic, and they had married in the following spring. Her husband, Oliver, had died three days prior to my chance encounter with his widow on the Central Plains. At that moment, he was riding off to glory in the baggage car at the end of the train. She hoped he wouldn't spoil.

"It was cold in Springfield, where Oliver passed while visiting his sister," she said, the disembodied words floating through her veil. "The freight agent didn't believe it was necessary to pack him in ice. He should keep till I can get him into the winter vault. Des Moines will be bitter, the ground frozen solid. He'll have to wait till spring thaw. Oliver was not patient." From the tone of that remark, I'd have said she was smiling. "He was a good man, although far from perfect. He taught woodworking at the Iowa Industrial School for Boys. He swore, but not above average. He played cards, but only for jingle money. He hit me once and once only, because I hit him right back with a darning egg in my fist. We raised two children, a son and a daughter. I was happy for a good many years before I became unhappy. I expect God will allow me a space of time in which to be happy again before I die. When it comes, I hope to be out of my mourning clothes. It wouldn't do for people to see me smiling while I'm in black. You know what people are like."

"I'm not going to sell you a blessed thing!" he declared, handing me his card. "No sir, not even if I knew for a fact that you won't be with us tomorrow. I'm on vacation, you bet! I'm heading for Yankton to shoot whatever the hell they got up there. I'm no Hiram Berdan, mind you, but I'm a good enough shot to put meat on the table, if your idea of table d'hôte is squirrel and possum. It ain't mine! What I love is a thick steak swimming in its own blood. You want to talk about life insurance? I took out the deluxe policy on myself before I left on this little jaunt. Why, I could get soused and drown in a bathtub, and Ida would be tickled pink by the payoff. She'll make a handsome widow, I'll tell the world! You see on the card that I'm associated with the Carolina Life Insurance Company. Here's a fact: Jefferson Davis himself was president of the firm right up until the panic of '73. Been dead for some time now, of course. Another fact: The blue bellies didn't catch him dressed in a woman's clothes

Eden's Clock 209

as he was leaving Richmond; it was only a black shawl of Mrs. Davis's sent him by her colored woman so's not to catch cold. People always tell stories to suit themselves!" He paused to draw breath before continuing his palaver. "I just came from a Lost Causes celebration at the North Alton, Illinois, Confederate cemetery. 'Soldier rest! thy warfare o'er, / Sleep the sleep that knows not breaking; / Dream of battlefields no more, / Days of danger, nights of waking.' That's what it says above the gate. It's by Sir Walter Scott, don't you know."

"My godchild, Gladys, was at the Iroquois Theatre three years ago to see *Mr. Bluebeard* and that funny man Eddie Foy. The thirtieth of December, 1903. What an awful, awful day that was! Six hundred souls perished in the fire—most of them, women and children, there for the matinee. She wore the new frock I got her at Marshall Field. She was so happy Christmas morning when she tried it on. What a pretty thing, my Gladys, just turned sixteen the month before. The muslin curtains caught fire from a sparking arc lamp. The owner claimed the building was fireproof. It said so in the newspaper ads. The show was to have been a New Year's treat from her mother." She sighed. I dared not turn around in my seat to see the author of that sad tale and the source of a sigh that told of a sorrow almost

210   NORMAN LOCK

past enduring. "All Chicago mourned," she went on to say. "Gladys's mother died, too, on that afternoon, and I lost the child I might have mothered in her stead."

A black man sat with his hands on his knees. His hands were big, his coat and trousers worn, his wiry hair and beard gray. He gave the impression of someone sitting in a church pew, conscious of God in the house. He was a powerfully built man who did all he could to make himself appear less so. A woman of middle age, who would have been considered a fashion plate in Oshkosh or Prairie du Chien, stood in the aisle and, making a gesture with which you shoo a cat, let it be known that the Negro should surrender his seat to her. The man said no in a tone that was neither defiant nor polite. She turned to me, and I lowered my eyes. "Is there no man here who will put this darky in his place?" I glanced up in time to see two white men haul the black one from his seat and evict him from the train car, while a third followed with the Negro's valise.

I pictured the hell Lilian would have raised had she been there. She'd have excoriated the bigots. She would have skinned them with her razor-sharp tongue. As a suffragist and reformer, she was tough as nails and fearless besides.

Without a voice, there was nothing I could do.

Eden's Clock   211

He sat quietly, his hands folded in his lap and his eyes staring straight ahead. He might have been in church, if not for the gray trousers and shirt and a coat of the sort that you see in the streets of small towns, worn by Union veterans of the Civil War. Hatless, his large head was crowned by thick gray hair. Here and there, the scalp showed where the barber's hand had slipped, or so it seemed. I thought his stillness unnatural. Even when the train swung into a curving section of track and the sun shone on the side of his face, he did not flinch.

The conductor paused beside him, asking for his ticket. The seated man looked into his hands, as if he might find it there. A man beside him handed up two tickets, and the conductor walked on.

"He's been in the asylum at Mendota," he said. Embarrassed, he may have felt that an explanation was in order for the other's silence. I, who was always so, needed none, but he went on just the same. "I'm taking him home to live with me and my wife. We have a small farm near Ames. I'm his brother, you see, and I think it will do him good to be with his own people again. He's been away nearly fifteen years. He's better now, or they would have kept him longer. They had him making martin houses. I fixed up a corner of the barn, where he can make them, and maybe a little money besides; leastways, it'll keep him busy. He's harmless, or they wouldn't have let him go. He hasn't said a word since he left Mendota. It makes me think of the milk bottle where I keep my spare nails and bolts; I turn it upside down, and they get stuck in the neck. I think of my brother being like that bottle, stoppered up. All he needs is a good shake. He always used to have a lot to say for himself."

When he got up to have a word with the conductor, his brother, who had not spoken since Mendota, looked out the window and said, "As for these things which ye behold, the days will come, in which there shall not be left one stone upon another, that shall not be thrown down."

Somewhere between Des Moines and Council Bluffs, a fire could be seen blazing at the edge of the plain, up against the sky, whose clear blue dome was smutted by thick black smoke, which, as far away from the tracks as it was, brought tears to my eyes, as if in mourning for the Earth. How oddly moved we may sometimes be by remotest causes, which—turn them over in the mind as much as we like—have nothing in the least to do with us.

A rubber ball rolled down the aisle, and a child came after it. He stopped by me and gave me a look so

Eden's Clock   213

piercing that I thought he'd find the sadness where I'd hidden it. Solemnly, he offered the ball. Seeing that he meant for me to take it, I did. He gave me a second look, so unlike any I believed a child capable of that I had to turn away. I kept the ball on my lap, fascinated by the stars with which it was decorated. It was an ordinary blue ball covered in gold stars, yet I did not take my eyes off it until the train began to slow and the boy was standing beside me once again. I understood that he wanted the ball back, that I'd been given the use of it temporarily, that it had been only a loan. I parted reluctantly with it. Without a word spoken, he joined his parents in the car's vestibule as the train came to a full stop.

"Council Bluffs!" shouted the conductor.

Some Pawnees were on the station platform. I had not seen a more dejected assembly of Indians since Buffalo Bill's Wild West parade on Fifth Avenue in 1901. Those I saw from the window of the train, on that cold day in Iowa, reminded me of my uncle's collection of stuffed birds, molty, bedraggled, and forgotten in the attic room above his shop. The motley crew held brass instruments at the ready. A long-haired white man, wearing a campaigner hat and an old Union army coat, got on a crate and then up on his toes. He lifted a baton, paused, then dropped to his heels at the same time that he brought down his arm. The band lurched into a medley of patriotic

214   NORMAN LOCK

ear splitters. Commencing with "President Garfield's Inauguration March" and ending with "President Garfield's Funeral March," the band rehearsed the tragic nature of every human life.

The Lord God, she said, had invaded her and would not let go His hold. She was proud of being possessed by the Holy Spirit, she admitted, but also frightened. It would not do, she said, to walk the streets of Kansas City with her eyes ablaze and her chest heaving, as if divine inspiration had supplanted the ordinary work of the lungs, leaving her breathless. And her husband, what would he think, seeing her so caught up?

She had been at a revival meeting in Sioux City for three nights running, in the company of her sister Sharon Rose, who was a resident there. She had never been so taken by a preacher's exhortations and visions of the life to come for the blessed. She had not been a religious woman, but by the third night, her soul was on fire and her cheeks burned and her throat ached, as with sickness. She wanted, above all, to be one of the blessed. All the while she talked, she did not seem to notice that I made no reply. I might not have been sitting beside her, so indifferent was she to everything in the train car, except her

Eden's Clock 215

exaltation, which she treated with the caution of a child engaged in an egg and spoon race.

"I'm from Kansas, which has the distinction of being bone-dry, a regular Mojave Desert. Why, a man can go crazy with thirst! But at the Sam Wilson residence, he can always find something potable. I get my stock from across the river in Missouri, which is as wet as Noah's flood." I noted a Masonic ring when he snapped his fingers for emphasis. "It arrives by boat, packed in excelsior, hidden among sheet metal and cast iron. I manufacture stoves." He was drinking from a flask. "The glory days are finished." He pulled a face indicative of contempt softened by the melancholy of remembrance. "Friend, I have seen the elephant." He tipped back the flask, emptying it of gin. "Sometimes two of them! I was tender as veal when I came out from the Altoona coal fields in '70 to soldier at the old fort—just a few years after the Buffalo Soldiers beat the Cheyenne at the Saline River. Those black fellas knew how to kill Indians! With their buffalo robes, woolly heads and beards, they scared the lice right out of their feather bonnets. Leavenworth hasn't been the same since the government turned it into a jailhouse for fleecers, murderers, and union troublemakers."

The old man didn't budge when I closed my eyes,

216   NORMAN LOCK

in the hope that he would move down the aisle to the empty seat next to a man engaged in paring his nails. Perhaps Mr. Wilson was enjoying the novelty of talking to a mute. "Friend, the Great Western Stove Company is a thing to wonder at! I write my own catalogues and such. Fella came all the way from St. Louis to shove his advertising firm. I showed him the door and told him to beat it." He handed me his card. "If you're ever in Leavenworth, look me up. I'll treat you to a swell feed and all the liquor you can hold."

Sitting snug against the window, she seemed intent on making herself small, as though to escape notice. But her muffled weeping showed on the face of the man beside her. Putting a cigar in his mouth, he went through the communicating door that led to the vestibule at the rear of the train. Still she did not leave off her weeping.

Knowing that the catalogue of human sorrows contains many entries, I could not guess the reason for her tears. Lilian had rarely cried, leastways not in my presence, but I remembered a night when, waking with a terrible thirst, I had gone downstairs in the dark to get a drink of water and found her crying at the kitchen table. What comfort could a silent man give? I crept back upstairs and got into bed. Many years later, she asked why I had turned away from her.

Eden's Clock 217

You see, I thought that she had not seen me standing, uneasily, in the doorway. My desertion became my sorrow, one of countless others.

To have had a reason for my speechlessness other than a chance encounter with a metal scrap, to have taken a vow of silence, like a monk . . . No, I liked a woman in my bed. Lilian, there never was another. How did they feel, my wordless embraces? Cold, I shouldn't wonder. Words are part of it—aren't they, Jack? Passion can open a clenched jaw and make a quiet man chatter.

12

Outside Ogallala, Nebraska, south of the big lake, we came off the rails. A freakish snowstorm had blanketed the county. We put up at the Crystal Palace Hotel until a crew could dig out the wayward cars from the drifts and lever them back onto the tracks. To justify its name, the hotel's owner had installed a chandelier, whose dusty glass pendants time had yellowed. The spittoons, however, were kept at a high polish. The barroom floor was scarred by the spurs of cowboys who had come in from the Platte Valley for a drink and a dance and, if they hadn't been cleaned out by cardsharps, a bounce on one of the upstairs beds.

Resting on one ungraced by a female presence, I was shivering underneath a blanket so unpromising

218   Norman Lock

that even the bedbugs had passed on it. In such blankets are dead men wrapped, after having breathed their last in a poorhouse or an asylum. After a while, the impression of something being softly said or sung grew on me, until I became aware of a muttered voice on the other side of the wall. I couldn't make out the words, and I thought at first that its source might be an Edison talking machine. I'd heard May Hyers sing "Ben Bolt" in a phonograph parlor on Broadway. What a gift to the mute! On the steamer back up the Hudson River, I pictured myself in my shop, listening to voices I had neither reason nor obligation to answer. Ever the practical one in our union, Lilian scotched that daydream by citing dollars and cents.

All that was beside the point once I'd held a water tumbler against the wall and pressed my ear to the bottom of the glass. The voice, I knew then, came from a flesh and blood mouth and not the tin horn of a phonograph. Immediately, I regretted having given curiosity its head, because I couldn't decide what I should do in answer to what was plainly a woman in distress. After a nerve-racking time that might have lasted five minutes or twenty-five, I went into the hallway and stood at my neighbor's door, hardly daring to draw breath.

My heart in my mouth, I knocked. The rap of my knuckles might have cracked the door and set the ersatz crystal chandelier chiming and every dog in town baying in alarm. I opened it slowly. Sitting on a caned chair, a young woman held a rag doll to her bosom and crooned what I took to be a lullaby in one of the Scandinavian tongues. If not for her breasts, which showed inside the unbuttoned dress, she could have been a girl playing mother to a doll. Her feet and hands were small, her features pleasantly arranged on a wide face. Her red-rimmed eyes and dirty, unpinned hair, however, ruined what would have been a simple, unaffected beauty. Poor woman, she was clearly mad. I closed the door softly, afraid that she would turn her distracted gaze on me.

I went downstairs and, in my fashion, asked the landlord about the young woman.

"She lost her child to diphtheria, then her husband, and then her mind. The pastor of the Swedes' church sent word to her brother, and he wired money to look after her till he gets here. He's somewhere back East; Cincinnati rings a bell. Terrible shame. They'd only just come west two years ago."

I went back upstairs to my room and heard, once more, the thin voice rising and falling on the other side of the wall.

"It won't last," I would like to have told her. "The pain will weary of itself and cease to gnaw." But she wouldn't have listened, nor should she have. To grieve is the last gift we can give those we love and who have ceased to be, and when grieving stops, as it must, that is the final betrayal.

When a heavy branch from a blighted elm tree crashed onto Lilian's cucumber frame, I replaced the broken panes with old glass-plate negatives that Mrs. Garman, abruptly widowed by her husband's burst appendix, had sold at ten cents apiece when she disposed of the contents of his studio, prior to moving to Elmira to live with her niece. I'd thought they might prove useful in the aftermath of a storm, such as peeled slates from the Kopfs' Dutch gable roof and drove the Albany ferry onto the flats. Each October, when Lilian would put away her garden for the winter, I would see how previous generations of the town's substantial citizens had become less so after the summer sun scoured the glass negatives, bleaching the light-struck silver particles composing the Walgroves, Coopers, Frasers, and Oliphants, stiff-necked, collared, brushed, and dressed in their Sunday best, until the day came when their graven images, like their shadows, had followed them into the everlasting silent night.

13

The train, which the snow and ice had set at defiance, was returned to the tracks. I took the seat I had sat in since Omaha and waited to be enlightened or

Eden's Clock 221

entertained by the other passengers. You could argue that I was no better than an eavesdropper, and I suppose you'd be right, Jack. But you scribblers aren't any better, for all that you may plead the exalted purpose of your calling.

He brought snow in with him on the toes of his boots and the brim of his Boss of the Plains Stetson, and on his wool coat, I smelled the cold of open air. He took the seat next to mine, stretched his long legs in the aisle, and squinted at me, as if he had been a long time in a place ringed by distant horizons. After a silence, he said, "I'm heading to Salt Lake City to bring my old man home. He's been locked up in Sugar House Prison for nine years."

He did not expect me to reply, and I kept my notebook and pencil in my pocket.

"They say he killed a man with a hoe. Maybe he did, maybe he didn't. He never said one way or the other." He examined his knuckles, which were large and swollen, and then he cracked them. I was surprised by how loud a sound they made in the passenger car. "They let him out a year early 'cause he's dying. I thought I'd take him home and let him wait it out there."

My father came to me, the thought of him, along

222   NORMAN LOCK

with the memory of snow and the winter that he took me ice fishing on Lake Saranac.

We rode in and out of clouds, or so it seemed to me as the wind stampeded them across the plain like a herd of buffalo and their shadows swept through the inside of the moving car. He was my age or a little older. His hat was on his lap, and from time to time, he turned it over and looked inside, as though what he had lost might be found there. He began to talk, not to me; at least he didn't acknowledge my presence with a glance or a nod. He talked to himself, his voice low, but distinct and even. Had he told his story before, sitting on trains, streetcars, or barroom stools? I guessed that was the case. The words sounded oddly flat, like a speech that had been rehearsed until wrung dry of sentiment.

"I lost my wife six months ago. What a funny thing to say! As though I could find her if I went looking. I sold the house, along with every stick of furniture and picture frame. I gave her clothes to the mission for the poor and needy. Now I'm going to work in my son-in-law's store. My daughter cleaned out a room at the top of it, where I'll live. Mind you, they're not doing it out of charity, since I know a thing or two about hardware. For a time, I pitied myself. Now I pity them, saddled with an old man,

Eden's Clock   223

though I intend to make myself useful. My son-in-law doesn't have time for the boy, my grandson. I'll teach him to catch fish with a fly and a spoon. I'm not a bad shot, either. I'll do right by them—see if I don't."

I thought of my daughter's wish that I should live with her and her husband, Peter, in Ohio until my time ran out. I smiled to hear again her childish voice singing Henry Work's old standard of the fire company parades, "Grandfather's Clock":

> Ninety years without slumbering
> (*tick, tick, tick, tick*),
> His life seconds numbering,
> (*tick, tick, tick, tick*),
> It stopp'd short—never to go again—
> When the old man died.

> *"Fred."*
> *"Who's there?"*
> *"Bonaparte."*
> *"Where are you, my friend?"*
> *"In Cuba."*
> *"Did you find what you were looking for?"*
> *"They hanged me."*
> *"I'm sorry to hear it.*

224   NORMAN LOCK

"At least now I know my real name."

I woke to find that the woman who had been sitting beside me since Salt Lake City had gone, leaving her newspaper behind her. I looked through the evening edition for April 14 of the *Deseret News*:

> Standard Oil announced today an additional advance in the price of refined oil and gasoline of half a cent per gallon . . . The Metropolitan horse racing season opens today at the Aqueduct track in New York, with the ten thousand dollar Carter Handicap . . . Mount Vesuvius is surrounded by a thick cloud of smoke, but ashes have almost ceased to fall. Many Americans, including passengers on the White Star Liner U.S.S. *Cretic*, visited the Vesuvius region today. Italian *carbiners* tried to prevent them from going farther up to the observatory, saying that it was not safe . . . Chicago millionaire celebrates his birthday . . . Two innocent men were lynched in Springfield, Missouri. Maybel Edmondson declares positively that Duncan and Copeland, both black men, were not her assailants. Negroes who fled into the woods are returning. Governor

Eden's Clock   225

> Hoch of Kansas condemns the hyena-like
> spirit of the mob . . .

Although I had dreamed of Bonaparte, and knew it for a dream, I feared to find his death notice among the items.

"I was all for it then, and nothing since has changed my mind. Burch said he'd shut down the Bunker Hill mine and keep it closed for twenty years before he'd let the union tell him what to do."

"He's a hardheaded bastard; I've no argument with you there. But what good did it do the miners to walk out? No damn good at all! And to pile on the agony, they went and blew up the mill! That stunt cost the W.F.M. plenty of sympathizers and donations to the strike fund."

"Workers and ranchers cheered when the train went by—'lustily,' it said in the papers."

"What do papers know? And even if a bunch of ranchers and track walkers cheered their heads off, what about Washington? Did they stand up in the marble halls and cheer lustily? Did the jackasses and the elephants toss their high hats for the Western Federation of Miners? Did McKinley send 'Big Bill' Hayward a valentine? Reds and anarchists is what most people think of them."

226   Norman Lock

"McCullough, you don't know cowpat from baked apple! The Burke Canyon miners had every right to strike the Bunker Hill, after Burch fired all the union men on his payroll."

"Seventeen men, he fired! They didn't have to go and wreck the whole shit and caboodle for seventeen men."

"A thousand men were riding the 'Dynamite Express' by the time the train reached Wardner. They weren't no 'handful' of reds and anarchists."

"What kind of union steals a train and blows a mill to hell with three thousand pounds of dynamite? And kills one of its own while it's at it?"

"When men's backs are to the wall, they'll throw dynamite sticks as easy as horseshoes."

"All your spiels concerning universal brotherhood mixed in a pot with sermons by Upton Sinclair and Clarence Darrow won't budge a greedy son of a bitch or fill a hungry family's belly."

Your name, Jack, deserves to be spoken in the same breath with Darrow's and Sinclair's.

14

When I opened my eyes after a nap, Edith Weller, the malcontent of Prairie City, Iowa, whom I mentioned at the start of this reminiscence, was attempting to lift her Gladstone bag onto the baggage rack above

Eden's Clock   227

my head. I unfolded from my seat by the window and helped her heft it.

"Thank you. May I?" By the turn of her head and direction of her glance, I understood that if I had no objection, she intended to sit beside me. The car, I saw by a glance of my own, was otherwise filled with passengers pursuing various occupations suitable to a confined space: peering at newsprint, scribbling in notebooks, tinkering with watches, conversing in loud voices or whispers, staring out the window in boredom or in thrall to perpetual motion, or sleeping. In one instance, an old woman had fallen asleep over her knitting, and the ball of wool had paid out a length of bright red yarn down the aisle.

I replied to the question just put to me by patting the seat, which I immediately realized was indecorous. She took no notice, yanked her clothing into place, and sat. I was gratified by the simplicity of her hat: Not a single bird had been martyred to adorn it.

"I've been riding in the rear car since Des Moines. I'd be there still, except for a party of teeth pullers that came aboard at the last stop on their way to a convention. If I hadn't scooted, I would have been asphyxiated by their stogies."

I liked her breezy manner.

"Will you be going on to San Francisco?" she asked.

YES.

228   NORMAN LOCK

"So will I. I have a ticket to hear Enrico Caruso sing at the Grand Opera House on the night of the seventeenth. Can you imagine my excitement? If I could sing, I'd shatter glass!"

Before the war, I had a good tenor voice.

"Shall we ride in together?"

IF YOU LIKE. MY NAME IS FREDERICK HEIGOLD.

"Mine is Edith Weller, resident of Prairie City, Iowa."

I smiled and signed, after a fashion, that I was pleased to make her acquaintance, and was suddenly aware of my broken tooth.

She spoke enthusiastically about the arts, to which she was devoted, although they were scarce as hen's teeth in Prairie City. Once a year, a traveling company from Chicago performed a Shakespearean play from which sex had been strained, like milk curds through cheesecloth, by Thomas Bowdler's bowdlerization at the start of the previous century. Once a year, she and a friend traveled to Des Moines for a musical evening of Gilbert and Sullivan performed by the D'Oyly Carte Opera Company. In 1882, she had heard Oscar Wilde lecture on the decorative arts, during his American tour. She remarked drolly that the bolt from which she had been cut was not the run-of-the-mill variety in Prairie City. Together with three like-minded women, she attended weekly discussions of books at the house of a friend, who served applejack brandy and grenadine. They were presently working their way through Thackeray. Mind, Jack, I'm not wisecracking. I respect them for knowing that life is more than an annual Methodist picnic, a Lutheran Fastnacht social, or a Knights of Columbus Christmas dance.

The locomotive stopped to take on water by the Humboldt River, at Wells, Nevada. Edith and I got off to give our legs a treat. We walked a little way into the desert to admire the cholla cactus, whose spines the setting sun was turning into gold.

"How lovely!" said Edith. She was pretty, middle-aged, and outfitted like a woman of means in a midwestern town for a night out at the grange. Ten years earlier, her dress could have been seen in store windows along New York's Ladies' Mile.

The silence of the desert, which seemed, at first, absolute, was disturbed by concertizing insects and birds. Utter silence is a privilege given to the dead, whose ears are packed with clay.

"Have you never tried to speak since your injury?" she asked.

THERE'S NO POINT.

"When I was a child living on the river Platte, a Pawnee raiding party burned our farm, killed my mother and father, and took me with them. For eight months after the Buffalo Soldiers rescued me, I didn't speak a word. Why don't you try, Frederick?"

230   NORMAN LOCK

I shook my head. Had a mirror been handy, I'd have seen sadness and also a little anger.

"You've nothing to lose by trying," she said, persisting beyond what I considered decent.

I thought of the larynx as a machine for the articulation of sounds. The surgeon had told me that the machine was broken beyond repair. A clocksmith knows the meaning of irreparable.

What *have* I to lose? I asked myself.

Nothing. Hope had been extinguished on the surgeon's table. I threw back my head, shut my eyes, and tried to remember what words felt like being born in the back of the throat, shaped in the mouth, and coddled by the tongue. I felt only my Adam's apple bob. I swallowed saliva to oil the voice box, which I pictured being rusted shut. I worked the muscles of my throat with my fingertips, swallowed more saliva, and opened and closed my mouth. I would have looked like a fish gaping at the bottom of a boat, its gills like sprigs of red coral. I managed to produce nothing more than a gravelly noise.

My hoarse declaration of intent was answered by a whinny, bray, and whimper let loose from a deep-throated mule, which came slouching into view.

"Why, the poor thing!" said Edith.

Only once before had I seen an animal as pathetic as this one: when the milkman's horse had been metamorphosed, with the aid of a papier-mâché hump,

Eden's Clock   231

into a camel for the Dobbs Ferry Nativity pageant. The man who materialized out of the desert air, along with this shambling four-legged corpse, looked no better than his beast. He appeared to be old enough to have seen two or three elephants. From plug hat to mudscows, his outfit would have been purchased new during the heyday of shoddocracy in the 1860s.

"We shoot trespassers in Elko County!" he barked as he brought to our attention a distant cousin to the blunderbuss.

Edith spoke up. "We'll be on our way as soon as the train gets its fill from the Humboldt River."

He lowered his gun. "All this sand belongs to me, every particle of it. I staked it out and filed a claim, all right and proper."

As the sun climbed another rung, his face emerged from the shadow of his hat. It had the look of old shoe leather that, by some miracle, remembered its former condition as pigskin and continued to bristle on his cheeks and chin. I had seen such a face before, behind a hedge at the Willard Asylum for the Chronic Insane. It belonged to my cousin Seth, confined during the panic of 1873, when he lost his business and his wits.

"I came out for the Comstock Lode in 1860, along with my old man," said the prospector. "He died there with no silver to show for his busted gut except the buckle on his belt. I went on to Colorado for gold,

232   NORMAN LOCK

failed, and came back here to Nevada. Nothing ever panned out, not gold, not silver, until I struck the mother lode of sand, which you're standing on! I'm going to dig till there's nothing left but rock. Then I'll go home to Philadelphia, richer than Croesus. You bet I will! I can't stop to jaw." He began to move on, he and his mule. Abruptly, he halted, turned to us, and said with the pride of a master initiating an apprentice into the mysteries of his trade, "It's not given to everyone to discover his life's purpose."

Back on the train, Edith closed her eyes. By the light of the electric globes, I read a few of these pages, the record of my days and nights. They seemed to have multiplied as the journey from Dobbs Ferry unspooled from the bobbin of my life.

Was it Emerson who wrote that the present contains the past, just as a surgeon's needle leaves behind it a lengthening scar, each of whose stitches is a record of the thread's past? The rent can be mended, the flesh healed, but the scar remains.

15

I felt myself rushing headlong toward the end of the American continent. Nothing could be seen through the car window except darkness richly veined with violet light, the same quality of light that Lucius Clay had projected into the room where Lilian's coffin lay

Eden's Clock   233

waiting for the processes of eternity to commence in earnest. "The Illuminator," a German invention intended to impress mourners with an experience of the afterlife, had been praised in *The Sunnyside*, a magazine for undertakers, which had published Clay's professional opinion on the optimum concentration of formaldehyde in embalming.

I'm reminded of a dream I had at Goldfield, a railway stop on the southwestern edge of the Nevada desert. It shook me, Jack, almost enough to make me get off the train and take the next one headed east. But I could no more shake off the idea of San Francisco than a dog can a burr. I yearned to be, as Walt Whitman rhapsodized, "Facing west from California's shores, / Inquiring, tireless, seeking what is yet unfound . . ." My head resting against the window, I fell into the deepest sleep, where nightmares are stabled.

The train is blocked by one of the pair of cherubim who stand guard at Eden's western gate, locked against us ever since the first eviction. Dazzling in the rising sun, the cherub who looms above us is no pink cupid on a valentine, but a colossus armored in bronze. Bearing the "flaming sword which turned every way," he bestrides the railway tracks.

I walk toward him, mesmerized by the brazen light shining on his breastplate. Finding my voice, I step toward him, thinking that to address this fallen piece of firmament is the reason the power of speech has been restored to me.

"Why are you blocking the way?" I shout as one does to giants in order to be heard.

Either my voice is too weak to reach his ears or he has not troubled to learn a modern language. (In his appearance, he resembles the picture in my mind of a Hittite king.)

A second vast shadow sweeps across the desert and folds, like a shroud, over the train. It belongs to the gold-haired woman in the allegory of American progress, unspooling telegraph wire as she strides westward through the upholding air. A caboodle of swindlers and profiteers, cattlemen and speculators, evangelists selling Jesus and peddlers selling pots follows her. Bison and aborigines take flight before that awful juggernaut of commerce, sanctimony, and greed.

She lays aside the giant spool; it floats in the clear blue sky. Like a raptor bird, she falls upon the angel, blowing out the flame of his sword and tearing at his samite wings. They grapple on the desert floor. The angel's wings beat the sand dunes flat with so much heat and force, they turn to glass. Edith, the locomotive engineer, and I stand transfixed by that battle royal, bearing witness to a ferocity not seen on Earth since the sack of Rome, or, in our time, the Trail of Tears. On the morning of the second day, the angel expires, and the heavens fall silent.

"It is finished," says the engineer, taking off his hat.

Eden's Clock   235

"Yes," says Edith solemnly.

The colossus of the American West shakes her golden tresses into place, adjusts the Star of Empire on her brow and the folds of her Attic gown, and takes up the spool of telegraph wire as easily as a woman does a bobbin of thread. And lo, in the west, Eden's gate swings open on its rusted hinge! And there before us lies the valley of the Yosemite, luminous in full sunlight.

"The way is clear," declares the engineer, remembering his duty to the railway and to us, his only passengers. "We've lost time, which we'll never make up."

"True enough," I say.

"Oh dear!" moans Edith, doubtless thinking of Caruso.

Once more the train is traveling west in the wake of the blond angel of American Progress, who stepped from John Gast's painting by that name to aid in our manifest destiny, the small one of Edith's and my making.

Through the train window, I see the immense carcass of one of God's angels burning on the desert sand. I hear a sound such as a thousand exploding boilers would make. I shout for no reason other than to let out the terror mounting inside me, as pressure in a boiler is eased by a blast of a steam whistle.

Is this why I was given back my voice? I ask myself. To shout in terror at the end of the world?

Someone was roughly shaking me awake.

"Oakland!" said the conductor.

"Fred, we're here," said Edith.

236   NORMAN LOCK

The weary passengers were gathering their belongings.

Night had fallen. Yosemite was behind me, engulfed in darkness.

"Last stop, Oakland!"

16

At Oakland, we came to the end of the line. Edith and I left the train and caught a nine o'clock night boat across the bay to San Francisco. The young woman from Pittsburgh stayed behind at the depot hotel, where her aunt would collect her in the morning. Edith had missed Caruso, who was, at that moment, "in the mountains," together with Carmen and the smugglers, as the opera's third act unfolded. The turret clock towering above the Union Depot and Ferry House loomed in the yellow fog crawling on the Embarcadero. I would visit Herbert Wallace in the morning and tell him that I had washed my hands of time and its instruments.

Edith's spirits were low. "After coming all this way, it's such a disappointment!"

YOU MIGHT STAY AWHILE & TAKE IN THE SIGHTS.

She bit her lip and said with sudden firmness, "I want to see the sea lions."

TOMORROW, WE'LL GO BY STREETCAR TO SEA CLIFF. I'LL STOP FOR YOU AT NOON.

Eden's Clock 237

I walked her to Lick House, a modest hotel for travelers on Battery Street, a mile from the ferry depot. The street was empty except for a removals van parked in front of a two-story house. Was it there for a new beginning or an eviction? I wondered. Edith and I wished each other a good night.

Husband, what are you thinking of?

Nothing, dear, nothing at all.

See that you don't make a fool of yourself.

I turned back on Market Street and walked to the Palace Hotel. Although I doubted that, after all these months on the way from Dobbs Ferry, the reservation Mr. Wallace had made for me would be honored, I stopped at the front desk. As expected, there was none, nor was there a room to be had within my means, which were, by now, on the lean side of naught.

Mr. Heigold, it appears that the announcement of your retirement was premature, I told myself. Let's hope that Mr. Herbert Wallace has a clock deserving of your extraordinary talent. Otherwise, you'll be hanging by your fingertips to the slippery edge of the Pit, also known as a fifteen-cent flop in San Francisco's Tenderloin, followed by a breakfast of thin coffee and stale sinkers. Not entirely skint, however, you have sufficient capital for a modest tuck-in at the Palace Hotel bar.

The Palace Hotel Bar

APRIL 17, 1906, MIDNIGHT
SAN FRANCISCO

You lean back in your chair and stuff your large hands into your coat pockets. You size up each of your three confederates in the newspaper racket with eyes that, unlike theirs, have surveyed vast distances and alien worlds. You've seen the China Sea and the two-thousand-mile-long Yukon River. You have walked beside the Yalu and the bay of Yokohama. You have gazed on Manchuria, Russia, and Pyongyang. Your eyes are blue and penetrating and, at this moment, a little sad. You are one of the most handsome young men I've ever seen, Jack, and I wonder if, in the midst of your exuberant embrace of life with the vitality of "the blond-beast," you, too, are slowly dying. No, not this man! I tell myself. Death would never dare to stop for Jack London, who, at this moment in his history, is lighting an Imperial cigarette. I notice that your teeth are bad.

You put your forearms on the table and finish the story of your conversion: "Just as I had been an individualist without knowing it, I was now a socialist

239

without knowing it, withal, an unscientific one. I had been reborn, but not renamed, and I was running around to find out what manner of thing I was."

"What you are, Jack, is a narcissist," says the cartoonist from the *Examiner*, whose ill-favored countenance could make its image reflected in a shaving mirror flinch. "Moreover, I don't give a good goddamn if Mother Jones *did* kiss you on the cheeks in Faneuil Hall, in front of a portrait of George Washington! She and Emma Goldman can kiss my fanny!"

"Shut your ugly mug!" you growl, and in my fancy, I see you put your big hand around his throat. It would take little to crush his windpipe.

"What's more, you're a traitor to your race, you and your socialist pals!"

"I am first of all a white man, and only then a socialist!" you declare with the zeal of a Bible-thumper or a senator on the stump.

"Pipe down, you birds!" growls the barman.

The *Chronicle*'s man changes the subject. "Who's the better boxer, George Dixon or the 'Old Master'?"

"Joe Gans, no question!" you asseverate—a word that always makes me think of knives. "I read a swell piece about him by Tom Anderson of *The Boston Globe*. He called Gans 'one of the most wonderful fighters from a scientific view that the world has ever known. There is not a trick or point that he does not

Eden's Clock 241

know.' Even Sam Langford declared him to be the finest boxer who ever lived."

"You bet!" agrees the ugly mug, who has been penciling caricatures on the bill of fare.

"You're cracked, the both of you!" bellows the reporter from the *Oakland Bulletin* as a drop of hair oil slides down the side of his face. "Those shines don't hold a candle to 'Battling' Nelson!"

"Don't be a chump! Nelson won't go three rounds with the Old Master at the Goldfield fight in September," you say as you play with a small Kodak camera on the table.

"Barman, oysters, *s'il vous plaît*!" calls the *Chronicle*'s man to change the subject once more, or to show off his savoir faire.

"It's gone on midnight, and time you boys were crawling into your holes," grumbles the weary barman, gathering up bottles from the table. They clank in his beefy red hands like bells that have lost their tongues.

"Boys, Caruso's asleep upstairs," says the cartoonist, who, having downed one too many boilermakers, has defiled the Palace Hotel's linen tablecloth with an illustration of Mother Jones and the Italian tenor in the buff. "What say we treat him to a shivaree?" He might have been a schoolboy proposing to put a garter snake in the teacher's desk drawer or a soused mule skinner contemplating the ribbons on a fancy

242   NORMAN LOCK

woman's drawers. "Maybe he'll sing us to sleep, if we promise not to snore."

"Even the dead of winter, standing outside the walls of Pyongyang, watching tens of thousands of Koreans flee the Russian beasts and the Japanese beasts, beats listening to that macaroni gargle!"

"I'll take Gilbert and Sullivan any day," pipes up the *Bulletin*'s man, mopping his face.

Taking a cigar from his coat pocket, the caricaturist suggests, "Light up, gents, and we'll smoke the fella out."

"Oh, let the dago sleep!" says the barman peevishly. "You loafers, be on your way!"

You and your companions pay and leave the taproom. I do the same and step outside in time to see you shout good-bye to them. I follow you down the street toward the water. I keep well back. You are walking listlessly, your head bowed. It's late; no doubt you've had a long day, and you did put away a lot of beer. I wait for you to turn into one of the hotels on Market Street, but you walk on toward the Embarcadero. I think of things I'd ask you if only I could speak. Here you are, Fred Heigold, at the end of the continent, walking twenty yards behind a man who has seen life up close and understands it, at least well enough to write stories that are wise in the ways of men and women who are down to their last matchstick. Damn your rotten luck, Fred! (Once, I thought

Eden's Clock 243

to have banished it and all else that would challenge a universe of absolutes.)

The Union Depot tower clock hangs like an apparition above the inky blackness of San Francisco Bay. I wonder if Herbert Wallace has found another clocksmith to fix it.

You stop at the edge of the pier and look at the bay. I stop, as well. I'm not beside you. I keep a respectful distance. As the minutes slowly pass, each one a stone, I ask myself, What do you hope to gain, Heigold, standing in the fog and feeling foolish?

Suddenly, you turn to me and ask, "Have you been following the Princeton Tigers this season? Or do you favor the Yale team for the championship? I'd bet my uncle Spratt's back teeth that it comes down to Bill Roper's boys!"

I make a noise in my throat that a man might make dancing beneath the gibbet.

You grunt, kick an iron cleat screwed to the pier, and walk back the way you came.

Sleep overwhelms me, sudden and irresistible, as if a narcotic has precipitated from the fog. I stretch out on a bench set beneath the depot's sheltering eaves and tumble into a dream.

I am dreaming of a sea, still and lifeless. I've come from far away to be here, this place at the end of the continent. High above me, an angel is floating; his golden hair is dull in the leaden sky. He holds a flaming sword, and I'm afraid.

"I've been sent to mend the clock," I tell him, unfolding the telegram from Mr. Wallace.

"Time is broken," he says. His voice is curious, a mix of admonition and regret. "It is better left so."

"I can fix it," I say softly, insinuating with the air of a seducer.

He shakes his head, and his long hair moves from side to side—too slowly, I think, to be real. "Time is the destroyer of worlds," he replies gloomily.

The remark offends me.

"Time crept into the Garden through the unlatched gate and unpacked death," he says.

I notice a drummer's case like the one that belonged to McGlinn, lying open on the beach. As my eyes begin to water, the case grows larger. Squatting over it, I see hundreds of .38 Long Colt revolvers, which the U.S. Army used to subdue the Cubans and the Filipinos.

"I know nothing of this!" I tell him, kicking the case defiantly. "I'm only a man who fixes clocks."

"Here, too, death has been ample," he replies, scratching underneath one of his wings.

I smile to myself to think that he may have fleas, this being who appears so lofty.

A long shadow passes overhead, further darkening the gray sky.

"Look!" he commands.

I look at the sky and see there a giant thumbprint made by a million whorling passenger pigeons. I remember how lovely they were to watch, pecking at gravel spread along the ferry slip, pink-breasted, their thrusting necks blazed with vermilion.

"In his journal, Cotton Mather wrote of having seen a flight of them a mile wide, taking several hours to pass high above Salem," says the angel.

I'm not surprised that he should know so arcane a fact.

"Soon they will exist nowhere but in memory," I say, wondering if Harley is still on the run.

"Yes, it will be so," the angel replies matter-of-factly. His teeth are like two rows of tombstones.

I watch as the whorl unwinds and forms a black river of birds. They are beginning to flow across their aerial empire, when men and boys appear on the beach, and fire rifles and shotguns into the moil.

I see that the sky is empty of birds and that the sand is covered with their tiny carcasses.

I begin to shout into the birdless silence.

April 18–22, 1906
San Francisco

I AWAKE WITH A START as Earth is shaking itself to pieces. The moon is down, the sky still dark, the time half past five by the tower clock. Then I remember that it is unreliable and that I have come to set it right. Already, the great noise that was raised to the heavens by the convulsing planet is fading into echoes of itself. I shape my mouth to shout as I did moments before, but that was in a dream—I know it now. What good is a voice in all this uproar? If I spoke with the tongues of angels, or with the one given to William Jennings Bryan at his birth, I couldn't stop the city walls from falling. I recall a verse from the Book of Revelation, describing the world after the seventh seal was opened: ". . . there was silence in heaven about the space of half an hour." Early on the morning of April 18, there is a silence such as might be the overture to the end of all things, but it is soon broken by the shouts and cries of a multitude of consternated citizens, who will, today or tomorrow, be unhoused.

I reach the Palace Hotel in time to see Caruso,

248   NORMAN LOCK

wearing a dressing gown over his pajamas, as he hurries out the door. He carries an autographed picture of President Theodore Roosevelt.

The Palace Hotel is burning. I take off my coat and cover my face with it against the heat. Across Market Street, the Grand Hotel bursts into flames. Lower Market also has become an inferno, more ghastly than any hell painted on a cathedral wall and too vast for Dante's poem to contain.

Intent as we are on the terrible spectacle, we don't notice the drunk pulling a fox terrier after him by a rope. "Turn back!" two men standing beside me shout, but amid the fire's roar and the crackle of the seven-story pyre that had been, minutes before, one of the city's boasts, he is deaf to their warnings. He walks on just as the north side of Market Street explodes into towering flames that devour man and dog, while we three others turn and beat it down Montgomery. My coat, I notice, is singed.

We are aware of daylight because of the jagged shadows the ruins cast onto the streets, which are full of rubble. We keep our eyes fixed on the ground as we walk to keep from falling over bricks, roof slates, uprooted pavements, whole chimneys and columns, all sugared with glass. Market and New

Eden's Clock   249

Montgomery Streets are jammed with people, many still dressed in their nightclothes. When we do look up, we see fires burning everywhere. Because of the dust hanging in the sky, the shadows are pale. Tens of thousands of San Franciscans are stumbling like blind people in an unfamiliar house.

The crowd swells Market Street and its tributaries. As unrelenting drops of rain will assemble into a flood, we are gathered, by catastrophe, into a congregation of frightened souls that flows toward the Embarcadero, seeking, as one body, the ferryboats. The depot clock's heavy hands hang down, pointing to the number six as though no longer answerable to time, even time that slowed and sped at the wind's caprice. The great clock has become governed solely by gravity, which keeps men and women in their place.

The ashen sky turns black. I become separated from the crowd of strangers I'd joined to be less afraid inside a darkness that could be mistaken for midnight. By now the fire has reached the skyscrapers of the Financial District. The intense heat creates a cyclone that rips chimneys and sheet iron from the roofs. Heavy pieces are falling all around me. Caught in a whirlwind, I drop to my knees and crawl up Bush Street as far as Kearny, where, emerging from the vacuum, I am able to stand.

What use would a voice be now? I could not order the gas pipes to resist the titanic strain or, failing that, to mend themselves, nor could I command the fire pumps set in the foundations of grand hotels to do as they were meant. I couldn't summon water from the bay or call on God to send rain to quench the flames that are beginning to jump from one roof to the next or to send a great wind to blow out the cornices of fire. The firemen will be driven back, their brass engines rendered useless by broken water mains. The second angel that was left to bar the western gate has arrived to wreak a terrible vengeance. Have I come all this way to witness the catastrophe? Was I silenced so that I could not speak a word of it? As smoke rises above the seven hills, my voice would be that of a mouse begging Prometheus to take back his gift. Not even Milton and Melville, whose granite words paved heaven and roofed hell, could write the story of the coming conflagration. The fire behaves according to its nature, and the people whom it menaces behave according to theirs. Burning shreds of curtains flutter in the air like black butterflies.

At Bush and Kearny Streets, I help two young men break into Robinson's Pet Shop. We open the

Eden's Clock   251

birdcages and, with our hats, shoo the panicked creatures into the street. We also release several monkeys, which amble out the door in comical fashion. We are delighted with ourselves.

I walk on to Lick House, only to find it flattened. If I thought any good would come of it, I'd kneel on the broken bricks, as crazy as any Christian flagellant or martyr, and pray that Edith escaped the flames. This afternoon, I shall visit Portsmith Square, where the quiet dead are gathered, as though waiting for the funeral train to arrive. I hope that Edith will not be among them.

I wouldn't have paid five cents for anything left where the Woolworth's store on Market Street had been. The wreckage makes me think of the young woman I met on the train. After coming all the way from Pittsburgh, where her house had dropped into a coal mine, would she still be lively and pert? I hope that she is, at this moment, in Oakland, at her aunt's place, watching the smoke rise across the bay.

I am stopped by a fireboy who wants to know if I have seen any horses. I shake my head. He tells me that the horses bolted. The firemen can't get the apparatus out of the station without them. I'm struck by his calm manner, this boy of fourteen or fifteen.

252   NORMAN LOCK

Later, I see soot-smutched men pulling a steam pumper down a cratered street.

At Golden Gate and Larkin, I stop to eavesdrop on a pair of policemen talking somberly to two reporters for the *Evening Telegram* about the death of Max Fenner, the "Hercules of the Police." He was crushed beneath a cornice falling from the Essex Lodging House, at 138 Mason Street, while trying to save a woman cowering in the entrance. The correspondents make a note of the item and wish the officers good luck as they continue on to the station house. They get as far as City Hall when its eight stories of terra-cotta wall remember, so to speak, a previous life as clay and thunder to the ground, extinguishing forever the small fires within the ardent breasts of the two policemen.

"Keep to the middle of the street, Mac!" one of the reporters shouts to me as they stagger down Larkin Street, pulverized to its original bitumen.

People walk up and down, carrying this and that. Men yoked to doors torn from their hinges, piled high with what is left of their belongings, trudge amid wreckage of what was said to be, only the day before, the Paris of the West. Other men lie sprawled in the street, shot dead by soldiers from

Eden's Clock   253

Fort Mason or the Presidio, in summary justice for looting their neighbors' stores and houses. Earlier today, I watched other soldiers help themselves to brand-new shoes from a crate pried open on Market Street. I have reached the promised land of bilk and money.

At the corner of Third and Mission, I see you, Jack, standing on a pile of bricks that had been gathered into a wall by the hands of men and kept in place by gravity and mortar until a force greater than them both tumbled them into the street. You aim the Kodak at a third-floor parlor suddenly exposed to the gaze of a public that could not be any less curious. I expect that you see in the camera's viewfinder the framed picture of wooded heights, hanging on a papered wall, above an upright piano, which has caught my eye, as well. Had a sleepless woman been playing, softly, a song about unhappy love when, in a terrifying instant, the earthquake made love of any sort seem frivolous?

Covered by gray dust raised by a collapsed building, which, in his fervor, he did not bother to brush from his hair and beard, he looks like an angry prophet wishing everlasting damnation on us all. "I was within a stone's throw of City Hall when the hand of an avenging God struck San Francisco. The ground fell away like an ocean at ebb tide. Then came the crash. Tons upon tons of that mighty pile slid away from the steel framework."

I leave him to his ecstasy.

When they have carted away every last brick and building stone, will they find the second angel, the divine spark put out and his feathers bloody?

Or will it be that of the woman dressed in a white Attic gown, her long hair the color of gold dollars, who has reached, at last, the end of her westering?

I spend the night in Potrero Park, lying on top of a tin sign proclaiming the virtues of Swaim's Panacea for scrofula, rheumatism, ulcers, sores, boils, carbuncles, diseases of the spine, catarrh, and wasting. A woman beside me wears the fur coat she saved from her burning house on Nob Hill. I am amazed by her carelessness when she shows me an emerald necklace in her handbag. Earthquake and fire have turned treasure into dross. That the air is cold also amazes me. I would have thought the atmosphere had been brought to a boil by the holocaust. In our aching bones, we know that anything can happen to anyone of us. Moment by moment, we are only forty-eight seconds from disaster, the duration of the tremblor that brought the city to its knees. I watch two men exchange cards for businesses that have been lost. Like schoolboys, they laugh at the joke.

I stop for a shave. The chair upholstered in green-and-purple damask once decorated a dining room. I think that it does not look out of place here on the sidewalk. (How readily we adapt ourselves!) The barber shaves me cheerfully.

"That's all that's left of my shop," he tells me, pointing the cutthroat razor at the striped barber pole propped up by reddish building stones. I hear amusement in his voice, and also a hint of pride. He wipes the razor clean of lather on his pants and, tipping back my head, scrapes the bristles from my throat. I picture his expert hand slipping and my stoppered words spilling like pomegranate seeds.

Where have the rats gone? Except for a dead one held delicately in the mouth of a cat, I have not seen any since Wednesday. Shaken from their labyrinthine nests within the lathwork of the walls, spilled from falling roofs, driven from burning granaries, they ought to be everywhere underfoot.

"Rats are always the first to leave," I heard one man tell another. They held shovels and had stopped in their work amid the rubble to smoke. "They have a nose for disaster."

"And dogs," said the other man, who wore a streetcar conductor's uniform.

"That's so," agreed his partner as he tossed loose earth lightly from the end of his shovel at a nearby sparrow taking a dust bath.

All that is left of a house is a wall, a staircase, and a room at the top of it, where a woman stands, holding a basket of freshly ironed sheets. Thinking of Lilian, I want to call out to her to take care not to fall down the steps. But then I think that all that can fall has already done so.

Everywhere people are walking. I don't believe it is in despair or desperation but, rather, to *see* that they go from place to place, unable to stop themselves. They must look at what their eyes cannot take in, nor their minds, either. What is everywhere around them cannot be described. It must be witnessed, and for this reason, they walk. They are all beggared and deranged.

A woman stops me in the street. In her hands is a San Francisco street directory. "I'm looking for my house," she says gravely. "I can't remember where I left it."

Another woman is carrying an iron and an ironing board down the middle of the street.

Eden's Clock   257

Seventy-five cents is left of the money Captain Bock, overcome by the spirit of generosity, paid me for the pocket watch, over and above the cost of my passage down the Atlantic Coast. What would I not do for a cup of coffee? Hearing that a breakfast of bread, butter, fruit, and hot coffee can be had at the St. Francis Hotel, which escaped damage, I walk to Union Square. The lobby and dining room are mobbed with people dressed as if for Mardi Gras. Among them is Caruso, wearing a fur coat over his pajamas, smoking a cigarette, and muttering, "'ell of a place! 'ell of a place!"

On the morning of the eighteenth, the great tenor did not awaken to breakfast served on a silver tray, in a room fragrant with floral tributes and the sharp odor of fresh ink on newspapers praising his performance of the night before. No admirers will tip their hats and throw kisses and carnations along Market Street as a motorcar drives Caruso to the ferry depot for his departure. With nothing left of the Grand Opera House, except broken hills of scorched bricks and timber, the ghost of Don José has nowhere to gibber. Among the dead who heard Caruso, are there any whose last thought was of José singing *"Ah! Carmen! ma Carmen adorée!"* after slaughtering her with his dagger?

258   NORMAN LOCK

This morning, I saw a man carry a typewriter as he hurried down the street, an old lady a large birdcage with four kittens inside, a man a pot of calla lilies, tenderly, as he muttered to himself, a scrubwoman a new broom in one hand and a large black hat trimmed in ostrich plumes in the other. An ancient-looking fellow dressed in an old-fashioned nightshirt and a swallow-tailed coat was startled from a reverie by a policeman remarking, "Say, mister, I guess you'd better put on some pants."

They're burning horses on a beach southeast of Rincon Hill. The poor beasts are worked until they die, oftentimes where they stand, head down, no longer able to walk on. As the saying goes, they die in harness, which, in this case, is a statement of fact. They are worked to death because there is no other way to clear the debris. Because drinking water is scarce on the peninsula, and what there is must be brought in from the mainland, they also die of thirst.

The prevailing winds being easterly, the stench of burning horseflesh is blown over the bay. A soldier says, "They'll smell it in Oakland and Alameda, and I hope the stink spoils their dinner." He spits a brown stream of tobacco juice, which sizzles on a hot length of iron fencing used to grill the horses.

Voices are heard calling from underneath heaped stones, asking for water, water, or so it seems to me, who, voiceless, hears what the talkative do not. Again and again, I force myself to go on; if not, I shall lose my mind, so near my nerves are to breaking. I tell myself, You're imagining them, Heigold, and wonder if I am.

A hearse packed with men and women laid out like spoons in a drawer reminds me of the Clays of Dobbs Ferry and the elder man's pride in the progress of his trade. His Köhler cooling board and latest casket-lowering device would be useless here, where death is far too large to be tidied up even by scientific undertakers. Not even Durfee's Best can stop the disintegration of the flesh.

"I told him he could take what he wanted; the fire would take it all soon enough. He showed me a picture of himself, and a woman I guess was his wife. I expect they were hungry. 'Take what you want,' I said. From the sound of him and the way he moved his hands, I thought he must be an Italian fella. At first, he didn't understand me. I signed that he could take whatever he needed. He smiled then and took a can of peaches, a couple onions, and some tinned meat—stuck them into his coat pockets, said something I took to be 'Thanks,' and went out onto the street, where a soldier from the Presidio shot him dead.

"I ran out after him, cursed the soldier up and down. He showed me Mayor Schmitz's proclamation: 'The Federal Troops, the members of the Regular Police Force and all Special Police Officers have been authorized by me to KILL any and all persons found engaged in Looting or in the Commission of Any Other Crime.' The soldier shrugged when I shouted at him, 'The man didn't speak English!' 'No skin off my nose,' he said."

I look for a place to sleep and find none so silent and withdrawn as the vault of the Wells Fargo Nevada National Bank, at Second and Mission. The heavy door is open; the gold has been ferried to the mainland and put to bed in another vault to nourish the dreams of Croesus, Carnegie, and Frick.

In another life, guttersnipes sleep in an abandoned vault on Wall Street, waiting for an orphan train.

The anarchists may be right, Jack: Fire and the dynamite the soldiers are using to complete the ruins, so that walls will not topple onto passersby, may be the means of destroying what you called the "Social

Eden's Clock   261

Pit." It was for this, perhaps, that I came here: not to fix a clock, but to witness the birth of equality among men, to see the poor and downtrodden climb out of the Pit and breathe free air. Clocks may have stopped in Eden, but I'll be damned if I lift a finger to fix them, no, not even the least of them!

This morning, I passed by Raphael Weill & Company, at Post and Kearney Streets, the dry-goods emporium known as the White House. Fire had turned the facade black. On the pavement, an E. Howard clock stands above a wrought-iron stanchion. The hands were as if soldered to the clock face, concealing teeth that have ceased to bite, though time, imperious and impervious, continues to rend.

Have I been all this long while traveling to and fro, only to arrive at the end of America and find it burning? Was I summoned to witness the confounding of time, in the upending of the great city foretold by John Winthrop, not, as he supposed, in Boston, but in San Francisco, or was I brought here by a blunder—mine, or someone or something else's?

A flight of stone steps are flanked by a pair of sandstone lions whose shapes are worn and pitted, as if they had stood an eon on the Sahara, suffering blasts of red-hot air. The stairs go nowhere at all. People sit on them, passing the time of day. On an upper

262   NORMAN LOCK

step, a Chinese man is heating water in a pan placed over a fire of burning newspapers and pieces of wood that, in a previous age, someone painted the color of a robin's egg. Seeing him, I fall back to an October evening on the Hudson River, when other Chinese flew dragon kites from the deck of the steamer *Adirondack*. (Surely this man who is making tea is not one of them!)

Among miles of smoking ruins, dogs wander, seeking masters, some of whom are here, some in the hereafter. They have come back from the hills, into which instincts sharper than ours sent them fleeing for their lives. How great was their terror that they broke their ancient covenant with man!

On Dolores Street, a woman is wiping a saucepan clean of gypsum. I can see her plainly through a gap in the kitchen wall, where bricks have been shed. She is lighting a Sterno to warm milk for her baby, who is knocking a wooden spoon against the high chair in which she sits.

CAN YOU SPARE A LITTLE WATER? I write in a notebook covered in buffalo hide, picked from the ruins of a stationer's.

She offers me a cup of water. I step partway into the kitchen through the broken wall to take it. I turn around, startled by a policeman suddenly appearing behind me. I expect he thought that I had looting in mind. He pushes me aside and throws his large brassy voice through the gap. "Madam, put out the Sterno can, and if you light one again, I have to shoot you."

The pavement dropped five feet below Market. The cinched earth squeezed shut the steel slots, where the cars clutch the cable running beneath the street, wound by brute steam-driven wheels, as though steel had been no more than tinsel. I walk on to the ferry depot, only to find its south wall gone into San Francisco Bay. Hundreds of the dispossessed push toward the Embarcadero, dropping bundles and suitcases, birdcages and sewing machines in a mounting heap west of the tracks, where the Mission cars used to stop. The ferryboats are returning to the slips to begin the evacuation to Oakland. Edith is nowhere to be seen. The palm of my hand is burned. How lucky it will be if, in a tumbled-down drugstore, I find a jar of Molliscorium!

Rats have returned to downtown. Fearing bubonic plague, the health department has put a price of five cents on the head of each dead rodent brought to one of its collection centers. Rat hunters are required to soak them in kerosene for an hour to kill any fleas.

264   NORMAN LOCK

I watch as an older boy pays a younger one three pieces of penny candy for three dead rats. Here, I tell myself, is a Carnegie in the making—a young hero like Horatio Alger's Ragged Dick, a boy of large ambition.

High above McAllister Street, a manumitted monkey is capering in a steel cage undressed of its columns, cornices, and balustrades by the quake. The iron dome of City Hall sits on top of it. The monkey chitters and swings from girder to girder, careless of the twenty-seven years spent in its construction. A woman cast in bronze stands atop the dome, holding a torch aloft. If I could see her face, would she wear a frown or one of those inscrutable smiles women are said to show the world when they wish to keep their thoughts to themselves? (For a moment, I think that it was she, with her brazen torch, who committed this arson.)

A sudden cry wakes me. Lilian has tripped on the ruckled carpet runner at the top of the stairs. Slowly, she falls down the stairwell—floating more than falling—then lands softly at the bottom, with nary a scratch. "My!" she says. "I felt so very light."

Eden's Clock 265

The engine houses still standing are quiet. Firemen who did not fall through burning roofs or die beneath toppling chimneys are restless. The apparatus is useless without water. When the earth cracked open four days ago, the mains from the bay and reservoirs were broken. Engine House Twenty-six, at Second Avenue and Clement Street, will give a concert of Sousa marches tonight at Lafayette Park "to lift the people's spirits." I heard enough brass bands in my soldiering days to last a lifetime, and I hope to hear no more of them till the last trump wakes me in my grave.

What if it has been a lie and time does not go on forever and clocks, which I believed told its progress, are only mechanical cheats set in motion not by the stars but by the masters of men, so that those in the Pit will be put to sleep by the sound of *tick, tock*?

After the emergency hospital burned to the ground, the patients were taken to the Mechanics' Pavilion. I walk amid two hundred casualties lying on the floor, most from South of the Slot, an area allotted to factories, sweatshops, and the wooden houses of the poor. Few remain, except as ruins. I am relieved and also disappointed not to find Edith among the injured, most of them laid low by toppled chimneys, the ground south of Market unstable, and the construction poor.

266   NORMAN LOCK

A fire breaks in from the roof and dances in the rafters. The doctor in charge orders the wounded evacuated. We carry them outside on their mattresses and put them into motorcars. Beyond our reach, we must leave twenty of the dead to be cremated in a corner where they lie.

Later, I wash soot from my face, in water leaking from a reservoir flume.

At Fort Mason, men and women have already started on the dreadful process that will turn them into dust. What an awful passage flesh must suffer before grace can be bestowed! What manure words can spread! One can sicken unto death of the harangues of churchmen spoken on behalf of their Deity and the oratory of so-called statesmen signifying nothing. One can choke to death on pretty phrases that would persuade us that a corpse is only a husk from which the tenant soul has fled. I could hunt through heaven and hell for Lilian and never find a trace. (The Revered Winter knows the truth of our existence, if he is still among us.)

The corpses stink in the warm April sun, and a number of us who spent the night near the reeking pile have left at first light to try our luck elsewhere. We have ended up near the sea, to be as far from the catastrophe as possible. The captain of a sand scow

Eden's Clock 267

offers to take us north to Vallejo, on San Pedro Bay. I stay behind as the others go aboard, then drop down in exhaustion on the sand. "Facing west from California's shores, / Inquiring, tireless, seeking what is yet unfound . . ."

I remember the charm inside my shoe, given to me by the Edisto root doctor to ward off hags and haints. (I'd lost Lillie May's dried palm leaves long ago.) I unfold the creased and dirty newsprint and see a smudge of black ink.

I walk across the peninsula to Sutro Heights, only to find that Cliff House has fallen into the Pacific, and with it the hope that I would find Edith, unharmed, watching the sea lions disport themselves on the rocks. I do not think I shall see her again.

On the way back to Lafayette Park, where I'm rooming in a tent, along with two brothers who owned a haberdashery, I encounter a man sitting forlornly on what was the brick buttressing of St. Luke's Church on Vann Ness Avenue. By his collar and hat, I guess that he is its rector. I mistake the cause of his pain for the loss of his church. Could I speak, I would remind him that his God is everywhere, even here amid the wreckage, even in the Chapel of the Fallen with its plaster of Paris sheep. And then, seeing the swollen jaw and black eye, I realize that

268 NORMAN LOCK

his agony has nothing to do with his ministry, nor is it an unwitting imitation of Christ. It is a toothache on which his every thought is centered. That a tooth—not even so much as a tooth—that a particle of crumbling bone should obliterate all thought of man and God is remarkable. He is blind to the destruction heaped about him. He is no prophet weeping at the fulfillment of his dire visions; he is only a common sufferer.

He pays me no mind, nor does he notice the colored woman picking her way through the debris. She holds a framed picture covered by a handkerchief as solemnly as if she were about to serve the body of Christ to the faithful kneeling at the altar rail. For some reason, I think that it is her wedding photograph that she carries.

God must be a mute, who speaks not with pencil or chalk but with thunder and lightning, famine and drought, earthquake and fire.

The strangest of all the sights I've seen since the disaster is a man selling phonograph records from a tent on Mission Street, beside the pile of bricks that used to be his store. Tell me, Jack, if you can: Is this—I shrug like a coroner called to examine remains beyond his ken—is all *this* simply of an order of magnitude many million times larger than the death of my wife? Were they both the result of a snarl in time's thread? Were they accidents that flung Lilian down the stairs and cracked the foundation of a great city, or was something altogether monstrous seized with the wish to laugh or sneer at our undoing?

Other than the ecstatic doomsayer I met on Van Ness Avenue, I've heard no one raise a voice or fist against God or fate, the rich or poor. No one curses Mrs. Lewinski, recently of Hayes Street, from whose skillet a flame jumped onto the kitchen curtain and leaped into the street. No one in my hearing insists that she be hanged for the "ham and eggs fire," which destroyed Hayes Valley and much else besides of the city. I see no panicked crowds or lawless mobs. Bloodred anarchy has not been loosed. For now, the people are, in Whitman's word, *imperturbable.*

I used to think that the whole and entire interest in throwing a pebble into a pond was to see the ripples spread over the water till they reached the shore. I think now that it is the return of stillness to the surface of the pond that is the point of the exercise.

A white handkerchief flutters from a mound of rubble. Believing that someone is buried beneath it, I clear away loose earth and stones. I soon realize my

270   NORMAN LOCK

error, a result of aggravated senses not yet blunted. What I mistook for a handkerchief is a letter to Reed & Barton, silversmiths, stirring in a breeze:

> Messrs. Reed & Barton
> Taunton, Mass.

Gentlemen:

I saved all of the Sterling Hollow and Flat Ware, with the exception of a few flat ware samples in the trays beside my books, stock sterling and plated ware books. The plated ware, it was impossible to touch, as the flames were then upon us, and another truck at $1,000.00 a load was an impossibility.

By then, the streets were a pandemonium. Locking the office doors, we mounted our guarded load and started for the country out toward Cliff House. My house being in ruins, I knew not where I would land, but I kept the teamster going with a gun at his back until we were three miles out of town.

As our photo books were destroyed, I request that you forward me a line as soon as possible, W. S. Hollow and W. H. Hollow hotel photos, and regular W.H. stock photos. Address: E. H. Adams, c/o

Wells-Fargo Express, #151-24th Avenue, San Francisco, Cal.

> I remain,
> Yours truly,
> E. H. Adams

P.S. Here we are all paupers together, but we have our grit left.

Never before now would I have read another's correspondence, whether business or private, without permission. But discretion and delicacy of feelings do not pertain when all is lost. What is private when we live together in tents? What is left of business when all forms of commerce have been destroyed? Will the New World begin, at long last, in San Francisco? Is it to be the city on a hill, which John Winthrop foretold—*but three thousand miles west of Boston*, where the Puritans first made landfall? If it is, Mr. E. H. Adams can be depended upon to supply the flatware.

At a playground on Irwin Street, two men and three women dressed as if for a church social or a Chautauqua meeting are loafing outside a slapdash affair of tarpaulins, porch awnings, and a swath of imperial brocade edged with tassels. They sit on a curbstone, all but the oldest of the women, who wears

272   NORMAN LOCK

a peach basket hat and a bertha collar. By virtue of her seniority and girth, the matron of the little group occupies the only chair, salvaged from someone's kitchen. The two other women wear straws and shirtwaists, ideal for this warm April day. A man, a derby in need of brushing on his head, sits back on his heels. Another, dressed in a white shirt, holds an empty saucepan. He isn't begging, and I suspect that if I were to offer him a few coins, he would hotly refuse them. On pieces of cardboard pinned to the canvas tarp, a clown among the lodgers has hand-lettered signs announcing *Welcome to the House of Mirth . . . Furnished Rooms with Running Water, Steam Heating & Elevator . . . Ring Bell for Landlady.*

After a breakfast of coffee and mush eaten on a table in Golden Gate Park, I walk west along the greensward to the Pacific. At the ruins of Cliff House, I was too distracted by my search for Edith to take its measure. Now I want to know what it is to stand with a continent at my back—the weight of America bearing down on me, my spine electric, my tongue once more loosened that I may shout into a wind, which rises in the Orient, my rage and my rapture, my ears filled with the commotion of westward expansion: prayers, curses, shrieks, moans, the babel of a hundred languages, the noise of the whip,

Eden's Clock 273

bowstring, cannon, carbine, dynamite, and, always and forever, of trains clicking on the steel scars of progress stitched on the skin of aboriginal land. Besides, I promised to send Boone Whaley a postcard saying if the Pacific Ocean is blue. Tomorrow, I will go to the post office, one of the few buildings left standing, and mail it, along with a letter to you, Jack London, in care of *Collier's Weekly*. I have much to say that may interest you.

"Watch out, mister!"

A horse, crazed and riderless, is bearing down on me! I have just enough time to run my tongue over my broken tooth. . . .

I can't believe my eyes when I come upon the Reverend Winter and Bonaparte. They have put up a "she-bang," as we Union soldiers called the makeshift shelters where, between one slaughter and the next, we nursed our wounds or died of them. It leans against a solitary wall. (The house where domestic comedies and tragedies unfolded lies in ruin.) Nailed in the mortar between its bricks, a sign proclaims CHAPEL OF THE FALLEN. (Was it for this that Winter thought up the name?) The two men are giving bread and wine to all comers. No longer the body and blood of Christ, the erstwhile sacramental food fills and warms the people's bellies.

274   NORMAN LOCK

"*Fred Heigold!*" *calls Bonaparte. I think he is too cheerful for a revolutionary.* "*Hello!*"

"*I thought you were buried in a Cuban grave.*"

"*Like the Almighty, I am everywhere.*"

"*Amen!*" *intones the reverend, much in need of a shave and a general airing.*

"*More bread!*" *shouts the congregation.* "*More wine!*" *calls a man whose veins are on fire with vin ordinaire.*

How very strange it all is! I say to myself.

"*How very wonderful that what God created in seven days should have been destroyed in three!*" *says Winter admiringly.*

"*It is indeed,*" *I agree.*

"*It's good to hear your voice at last, my friend!*" *cries Bonaparte.*

"*I have put away my chalk,*" *I tell him, contented. From my coat pocket, I take out my letter to Jack London.*

Eden's Clock 275

Frederick Heigold
San Francisco, Calif.
April 22, 1906

Dear Mr. London,

I was sitting at a table next to yours in the Palace Hotel taproom the night before the earthquake, when you told the story of the Pit. After the bar closed, I followed you down Market to the Embarcadero. I was the man on the pier whose opinion you sought about the Yale and Princeton teams. When I didn't answer, you would have considered me unfriendly or rude.

Snug inside the remains of John Rantala's saloon, I drink a hot cup of Brandenstein & Company coffee, whose beans were roasted in this city not long ago. Outside Rantala's place, rich and poor alike eat at long trestle tables in the parks and squares, where they sleep in snowy white tents. Rich and poor getting along like Shakers and New Harmonites! How democratic a vista! This afternoon, I watched a nob in evening dress spoon soup into tin cans and cups for a family of tatterdemalions that likely had two rooms in a tenement house South of the Slot. Mr. London . . . Jack. I may have glimpsed not the birth of a new order but only the possibility that, one day, oligarchs shall dwell with plebeians and eat together of the fat of the land. In perfect conviviality, the scions of Carnegie and Pinkerton shall drink Mr. Brandenstein's superb coffee, along with the offspring of Emma Goldman and Eugene Debs.

I expect that Eden's clock will tick once more. Paradise will be postponed, utopia delayed, the dream deferred. But in a hundred years, we may become the nation foretold at our beginning: that of a people who "delight in each other; make others' conditions our own, rejoice together, mourn together, labor and suffer together, always having before our eyes our commission and community in the work, our community as members of the same body. So shall we keep the unity of the spirit in the bond of peace."

And no one living shall be without a voice.

Until that blessed day, we ride the juggernaut.

> ## Collier's, the National Weekly
> ### May 5, 1906
> # The Story of an Eyewitness
> #### By Jack London, Special Correspondent

Not in history has a modern imperial city been so completely destroyed. San Francisco is gone. Nothing remains of it but memories and a fringe of dwelling-houses on its outskirts. Its industrial section is wiped out. Its business section is wiped out. Its social and residential section is wiped out. The factories and warehouses, the great stores and newspaper buildings, the hotels and palaces of the nabobs, are all gone.

Within an hour after the earthquake shock the smoke of San Francisco's burning was a lurid tower visible a hundred miles away. And for three days and nights this lurid tower swayed in the sky, reddening the sun, darkening the day, and filling the land with smoke.

There was no opposing the flames. There was no organization, no communication. All the cunning adjustments of a twentieth century city had been smashed by the earthquake. The streets were humped into ridges and depressions, and piled with the debris of fallen walls.

Dynamite was lavishly used, and many of San Francisco's proudest structures were crumbled by man himself into ruins, but there was no withstanding the onrush of the flames. Time and again successful stands were made by the fire-fighters, and every time the flames flanked around on either side, or came up from the rear, and turned to defeat the hard-won victory.

On Thursday morning, at a quarter past five, just twenty-four hours after the earthquake, I sat on the steps of a small residence on Nob Hill. I went inside with the owner of the house on the steps of which I sat. He was cool and cheerful and hospitable. "Yesterday morning," he said, "I was worth six hundred thousand dollars. This morning this house is all I have left. It will go in fifteen minutes."

Eden's Clock 279

He pointed to a large cabinet. "That is my wife's collection of china. This rug upon which we stand is a present. It cost fifteen thousand dollars. Try that piano. Listen to its tone. There are few like it. There are no horses. The flames will be here in fifteen minutes."

Outside, the old Mark Hopkins residence, a palace, was just catching fire. The troops were falling back and driving the refugees before them. From every side came the roaring of flames, the crashing of walls, and the detonations of dynamite.

I walked past the broken dome of the City Hall building. This part of the city was already a waste of smoking ruins. Here and there through the smoke, creeping warily under the shadows of tottering walls, emerged occasional men and women. It was like the meeting of the handful of survivors after the day of the end of the world.

Eden's Clock   281

That night proved our closest to realizing a dream that came now and again to Jack in sleep, that he and I were in at the finish of all things—standing or moving hand in hand through chaos to its brink, looking upon the rest of mankind in the process of dissolution.

—Charmian London (writing about Wednesday night, April 18, 1906)

AFTERWORD

A common thread in all twelve books of The American Novels series is their author's perplexity that his country should be other than he imagined it in his youth. How is it, America, that, as late in the day as 2025, injustice persists in your racial, political, and economic relationships, in the treatment of "your tired, your poor, / Your huddled masses," and your conduct toward the Earth and the multitudes of other species over which we were, according to the creation myth, given dominion by the God of Moses or, if you like, the brutal wars of evolution? Why have you failed to protect what the "savages" husbanded and revered? Were they insufficiently evolved, to your way of thinking, and therefore unworthy of belonging to the American empire? When will you shake off your imperial ambition? When will we become, in the words of John Winthrop, whose writings began to forge the nation's social contract and origin story, a people who "delight in each other, make others' conditions our own, rejoice together, mourn together, labor and suffer together"?

284   NORMAN LOCK

Heigold's letter to Jack London, expressing a Whitmanesque vision ("Rich and poor getting along like Shakers and New Harmonites! How democratic a vista!"), does not mention San Francisco's Chinese, who, after the complete destruction of Chinatown, were segregated in a refugee camp at the Presidio/ Fort Winfield Scott. Many of the city's government and business elite saw, in the destruction, an opportunity to relocate Chinatown from the city's center to a less valuable and visible piece of real estate, such as Hunter's Point—or Oakland, whose residents stoutly protested against "the degradation, the filth, and the vice that a Chinatown means" (*The Oakland Herald*, April 27, 1906). In 1900, nearly fifteen thousand Chinese were living in San Francisco's Chinatown, compared to fewer than two thousand African Americans, who had been able to integrate into the general population because of their small number. More visible, the Chinese were the target of race hatred. (Mind you, the city's Blacks were largely excluded from the efforts of the city's official charity agencies in the post-1906 period.)

Jack London was, as is said to exculpate the racial prejudice of those of a past era, a man of his times, with all the faults of the men and women of the age. The wrongheadedness of that argument is apparent to us, if not to them. For all that I wish it were otherwise, London did say, after he was attacked for his radical

Eden's Clock   285

views at a political meeting in San Francisco, "I am first of all a white man, and only then a socialist!" (What will be said of us and our time a hundred years hence? What blame laid at the foot of our graves?)

I strive for fidelity, which obliges me to get the facts right as I call the past into being on the page. The ideas of another time, however, are not so easily rendered within the constraints of a dramatic narrative. Ideas, be they flawed, specious, or violently opposed to one another, are the mind of a nation. Because a nation is in a state of flux and contradiction, defining it is impossible within the covers of a single book. One chooses, from the welter of incidents, a viewpoint; I can only hope that mine will unsettle readers enough to make them question everything and take no single person's truth as absolute, not even my own.

"There was things which he stretched, but mainly he told the truth." So says Huck Finn of Mark Twain, and so I would wish to be said of me. If I told "stretchers," I was at some pains to make my prevarications known. I admit that Rebecca Salome Foster, the Tombs Angel, died in 1902, in a fire at her Park Avenue Hotel. On the other hand, Caruso *was* jolted out of his bed in the Palace Hotel by the earthquake, he did flee the hotel in his dressing gown, carrying a framed portrait of Theodore Roosevelt, and he was

286　NORMAN LOCK

heard to say of San Francisco, "'ell of a place! 'ell of a place!" Although Jack London reported on the earthquake and photographed the ruins, he did not interview the great tenor. The foiled plot to steal and ransom Abraham Lincoln's remains is factual, and there was indeed a journal for the funeral trade entitled *The Sunnyside*.

Founded in New York City in 1853 by Charles Loring Brace, the Children's Aid Society, its mission houses, industrial schools, and orphan trains rescued hundreds of thousands of young children living in misery and danger in the city's streets, areaways, subway entrances, coal yards and lumberyards, barrels, drainage pipes, and abandoned bank vaults. My intention is not to mock philanthropic enterprises in defense of children, but to condemn the conditions that bring them into being, as well as the subversion of their ideals by autocratic relationships, which are, sadly, with us. That children were preyed on, as they continue to be, is one of many unspeakable truths about humankind.

Eden's Clock can be said to begin with the death of Herman Melville (and American literary romanticism) and end with the appearance of Jack London, who, along with Hamlin Garland, Stephen Crane, and Frank Norris, influenced the literary naturalism of Sherwood Anderson, Ernest Hemingway, John Steinbeck, and much of the American literature written after them. London is far more accomplished a writer and complex an individual than many would now suppose, who believe him to have been a writer of adventure stories for boys. Granted, the writing is uneven; he lived beyond his means and wrote much to outpace his creditors. In the novel, London functions as a social conscience sensed beneath the text; in his brief span, he denounced, in public forums and published work, the inequities of American life, which are sharply felt in *The People of the Abyss* (1903), *The Iron Heel* (1908), and his numerous essays and speeches. In that these inequities persist in the present day and constitute one of the themes of *Eden's Clock*, it is natural that I should include Jack London to the extent that I have. My portrait is, of course, limited to a single facet of a multifarious personality.

I knew early on that Frederick Heigold's journey would end when San Francisco and the mythology of American progress were destroyed. That they were quickly resurrected and fortified, without advantage to the people of the abyss, is evident today in the vast homeless population of that other city on a hill, the City of the Golden Gate.

ACKNOWLEDGMENTS

In an age such as ours, when history is neglected, suppressed, or even rewritten to suit a narrow, prejudiced view, when truth is falsified, and a witness liable to perjury, writers, it seems to me, have an obligation to give notice to their readers of their adaptations of the historical record and appropriations of actual characters.

I could not have written *Eden's Clock* without the aid of online resources such as Chronicling America: Historic American Newspapers, the Library of Congress; Cornell University Library's Making of America collection; the David Rumsey Map Collection; the HathiTrust Digital Library; the Hudson River Maritime Museum; and the digital collections of the Library of Congress and the New York Public Library.

To make a start at understanding the brutal and imbruting conditions suffered by tens of thousands of homeless children in New York City at the time of this novel, I consider two books indispensable: *How the Other Half Lives: Studies Among the Tenements of New*

290 NORMAN LOCK

York, by Jacob Riis, and *Low Life*, by Lucy Sante. My education continued at these websites: The Bowery Boys: New York City History ("The Harsh Lives of New York City Street Kids, Captured—in a Flash—by Jacob Riis"); the National Orphan Train Complex ("Orphan Train Rider Stories"); the Noyes Home for Children ("Facts about the Orphan Train Movement: America's Largest Child Migration," March 3, 2016); and the Social Welfare History Project, Virginia Commonwealth University Libraries ("Child Labor in New York City Tenements," by Mary Van Kleeck, January 18, 1908). I am indebted to the Historical Crime Detective website for the colorfully idiomatic language that found its way into passages of the novel, taken from its "Criminal Slang Glossary: 1890–1919."

The mind of the age, warped by the effects of that other great depression, known as the great panic of 1893, is vividly portrayed in Michael Lesy's remarkable collage of photographs and newspaper reportage, *Wisconsin Death Trip*.

"Teddy on Color-Line" and "Crazy Millionaire" appeared in the *Richmond Times–Dispatch* of November 28, 1902. The items that Heigold reads in the Tombs were published in a November 1905 edition of the New York daily newspaper *The Sun*. The report on "Intercollegiate Socialists" was printed in *The Virginia Enterprise* (Virginia, St. Louis County, MI) on August 4, 1905. Items that Heigold reads in the rice

Eden's Clock 291

loft appeared in the January 16, 1878, *Press and Banner*, of Abbeville, South Carolina. The *Deseret News* he reads on the westbound train was published on April 16, 1906. All quoted text was taken, almost verbatim, if abridged, from the original sources.

"John Chinaman" was published in *The California Songster* (San Francisco: Appleton, 1855) and reached me by way of various internet sources. That defamatory song was popular during the California gold rush.

E. H. Adams's letter to Reed & Barton, silversmiths, concerning the restoration of his lost flatware samples and catalogues is authentic and, for me, symbolizes American virtues of self-reliance, initiative, and fidelity, as well as the greed too often associated with American commercial life.

The passage beginning "The tide was well up" is from a description of Edisto Island written by Thomas Wentworth Higginson, published in his book *Army Life in a Black Regiment.* Higginson was a Bostonian, a Unitarian minister, a militant abolitionist, a member of the Secret Six, which supported John Brown's insurrection, a man of letters, and, incidentally, the "Dear Friend" to whom Emily Dickinson sent her poems, asking him if he were too busy to "say if my verse is alive." He commanded the first regiment of freedmen, the First South Carolina Volunteers. I discovered the quotation in William S. McFeely's *Sapelo's*

292   NORMAN LOCK

People, which helped me understand, as much as a single book can, the complex agrarian society and history of the Sea Islanders. (For anyone interested in their contemporaries, I recommend the online newsletter published by Gullah Geechee Cultural Heritage Corridor Commission, located on John's Island, South Carolina.)

For Captain Bock's recollections of Winslow Homer, I relied on *Winslow Homer in the 1890s: Prout's Neck Observed*, essays by Philip C. Beam, Lois Homer Graham, Patricia Junker, David Tatham, and John Wilmerding, and also *American Painting of the Nineteenth Century*, by Barbara Novak.

To write the impressions intended to represent and simplify the extraordinarily complex course and aftermath of the disaster, I used the following articles published on the Museum of the City of San Francisco's website: "The Progress of the Fire in San Francisco, April 18–21, 1906"; "Synopsis of the San Francisco Police and Municipal Records of the Greatest Catastrophe in American History," by Thomas S. Duke, Captain of Police, San Francisco, 1910; "Timeline of the San Francisco Earthquake, April 18–23, 1906" (taken from Gladys Hansen's "Chronology of the Great Earthquake"); and "Eyewitnesses to the Earthquake and Fire," some of whose words salted my impressions. My fragmentary account was also informed by an item published by the San Francisco

Eden's Clock 293

Fire Department Museum, "Great Fires: 1906 Great Earthquake & Fire," written in 1906, and an essay in the *California Historical Quarterly*, summer 1976, "The California National Guard in the San Francisco Earthquake and Fire of 1906," by James J. Hudson.

Information on the refugees of the disaster, their housing, relief, and the discrimination with which some were treated was found on the website of the National Park Service, Presidio, San Francisco, California, "1906 Earthquake: Chinese Displacement"; in "Conflicting Definitions of Relief: Life in Refugee Camps after the San Francisco Earthquake of 1906," by Emily Neis, 2018; and in "Housing Reconstruction after the Catastrophe: the Failed Promise of San Francisco's 1906 'Earthquake Cottages,'" by Marie Bolton and Nancy Unger, in *Annales de démographie historique* 120, no. 2 (2010): 217–40.

Jack London's eyewitness account of the day and night of the earthquake is drawn from his much larger article commissioned by *Collier's, the National Weekly*. The piano and framed landscape that I have London photograph was suggested by Arnold Genthe's picture *Looking Down Sacramento Street, San Francisco, April 18, 1906*. A celebrated portraitist, Genthe, as well as London, was a member of the Bay Area bohemian group known as "The Crowd."

I have given Jack London his own published words to speak in the passage beginning "I found

294   NORMAN LOCK

there all sorts of men, many of whom had once been as good as myself and just as blond-beast" from "How I Became a Socialist," 1903. From that essay, I also quoted "Just as I had been an individualist without knowing it, I was now a socialist without knowing it, withal, an unscientific one. I had been reborn, but not renamed, and I was running around to find out what manner of thing I was." A few weeks before his death, in 1916, of uremic poisoning, London declared, "The white man is a born looter." He was forty years old. To learn more about this exceptional American, who experienced life—high and low—as few other writers have, I recommend *Jack London: An American Life*, by Earle Labor.

The quotation beginning with "delight in each other" and ending with "the unity of the spirit in the bond of peace" is from John Winthrop's "A Model of Christian Charity."

Art and Photos: (1) *Desolation*, from Thomas Cole's *The Course of Empire* series, in the Collection of the New-York Historical Society, object number 1858.5 (Gift of the New-York Gallery of the Fine Arts); (2) *American Progress*, by John Gast, 1872, from the Library of Congress, Prints and Photographs Division; (3) portrait of Jack London, 1906, Huntington Digital Library, Huntington Library, San Marino,

Eden's Clock 295

California; (4) "Scene painter amid earthquake rubble painting picture of ruins of large building after San Francisco earthquake—fire, 1906," the Library of Congress, Prints and Photographs Division.

From continental U.S. railroad maps of the period, I concluded that Heigold could have traveled from Willtown Bluff, South Carolina, to Oakland, California, by the following routes: (1) Seaboard Air Line Railroad (the designation Air Line was commonly used to denote the straightest route between two points) to Atlanta, Georgia, (2) Savannah, Florida & Western Railway to Jesup, Georgia, (3) East Tennessee Railway to Memphis, Tennessee, (4) Kansas City, Fort Scott and Memphis Railroad to Kansas City, Missouri ("Memphis Route"), (5) Council Bluffs [Iowa] and St. Joseph Railroad to Omaha, Nebraska, and (6) Union Pacific Railroad to Oakland, California.

Writing is a lonely business, as has often been said. Mine has been made considerably less so by my wife, Helen, our children, Meredith, Nicholas, Andrew, and Alexis, my cousins David and Nancy Moore, my friends Charles Giraudet, Kathryn Rantala, Edward Renn, and Marco Knauff, advocates Eugene Lim, John Madera, and Tobias Carroll, and my quite wonderful publisher, Erika Goldman, who helped me shoulder this book up the steep hill, to find there its form and final expression. I am grateful to her and to my other generous colleagues at Bellevue Literary Press: Jerome Lowenstein, M.D., founding publisher, Molly Mikolowski (for her promotion of the books and their author), Laura Hart (for her administration of countless details), Joe Gannon (for his book design and production oversight), Carol Edwards (for her rigorous copyediting), Alban Fischer (for his cover art), and Elana Rosenthal (for her meticulous proofreading). A descriptor cannot do justice to the labor and service to the books that pass through their hands.

Eden's Clock 297

Scene painter amid earthquake rubble painting picture of ruins of large building after San Francisco earthquake—fire, 1906

Bellevue Literary Press is devoted to publishing
literary fiction and nonfiction at the intersection
of the arts and sciences because we believe that
science and the humanities are natural companions
for understanding the human experience.
We feature exceptional literature that explores
the nature of consciousness, embodiment, and
the underpinnings of the social contract. With
each book we publish, our goal is to foster a rich,
interdisciplinary dialogue that will forge new tools
for thinking and engaging with the world.

To support our press and its mission,
and for our full catalogue of published titles,
please visit us at blpress.org.

Bellevue Literary Press
New York